cruel and beautiful world

KATRINA MARIE

prologue

I HEAR the party raging around me. Red Dirt Rock blaring from the speakers in the living room. The haze of smoke hanging in the air. I can't remember exactly where I am, except that I'm at some frat party. All I know is I'm in the bathroom trying to put myself back together.

I know better than to mix alcohol with my anxiety meds, but right now I don't care. I need to throw this whole "Little Miss Perfect" persona out the window. That's not who I am, not really. It's what I let everyone else see. The only exception would be Tonya, and she's not here to pick me back up again. Inside, I'm a mess. I'm filled with anxiety, insecurities, and an unbreakable need to self-destruct. I'm a ticking time bomb... just waiting to explode.

I remember when I was a child and had nothing expected of me. As long as I did well in school and stayed out of trouble, I could do whatever I wanted. I'm not sure when all that changed, but I wish I could go back to those carefree days more than anything.

I scan the bathroom trying to find something to dry my hands. There's mold in the creases of the bathtub, dried toothpaste in the sink and splattered across the mirror. You can definitely tell these are guys that don't care about appearances. I can only imagine what my perfect and pristine mother would say about the state of this space. Not to mention how the rest of the house looks, with cups and empty bottles scattered across it.

I feel another bout of sickness hit me and rush to lean my head over the toilet. I heave up everything that's left in my stomach. This is the *last* time I'll do this. I say that, but we all know this time next week, I'll be back in the same position.

Someone's banging on the door causing me to look up. I glance at the door, but another round of sickness hits me. They're just going to have to wait. I'm not moving from this spot, and they can't get through the door. That's when I hear his voice, and assume he's the one trying to get in.

"Cami," Travis yells through the piece of wood separating us. "I know you're in there. Open the damn door."

I blink my eyes, trying to process what he just said. For some unknown reason, Travis thinks he has to look out for me. He found me in pretty much the same state a week ago. Since then, he's shown up at almost every party I've attended. I don't know why he won't leave me alone. We aren't even friends. We have a few classes together. That doesn't make him my fucking keeper. Besides, he doesn't have much room to treat me like I'm a kid. Any time I've seen him, he's hanging out with the academic kids that dare to come to these parties.

I try to stand up...slowly. The bathroom isn't that big and it shouldn't take this much effort. Grabbing the sink for support, I turn to unlock the door. A wave of dizziness comes over me, and I stumble. I reach for anything that will help catch my fall, but my fingers slip off every object I attempt to grasp.

As the lights begin to fade around me, I hear Travis calling my name. "Cami... Cami." It sounds like he's out of breath. "Damn it, why do you keep doing this?"

And everything goes black.

cami

IT'S BEEN three weeks since I blacked out at the party, and I haven't been able to shake Travis. I swear he memorized my class schedule or something. He always manages to find me between classes I don't have with him. Two weeks ago he invited himself to my dorm to watch movies and eat popcorn. It's driving me crazy. The only reason I escaped him last weekend is because I went to visit Tonya after she gave birth to Layla. I'm not some fragile piece of porcelain that will break with the tiniest bump.

"I *seriously* can't believe this guy, Tonya." I'm practically hollering through the phone. "It's like he's freaking stalking me. What the hell am I supposed to do about that?"

I'm going to put a hole in the carpet with the amount of pacing going on, but I can't be still. I have to do something. It won't be so bad if I calm down, but I can't. Travis has an effect on me, and I can't tell if it's good or bad. Is the carpet fraying, or is that my imagination running wild, yet again? My parents won't be thrilled if they have to pay for damages.

Tonya sighs on the other end of the receiver, "First thing, girlfriend, you need to lower your voice. I'm pretty sure you are going to wake Layla up with all that screaming." I hear the soft whimpers of my Goddaughter, and that sound helps me calm down. Not all the way, but enough that I can talk in a semi-normal voice.

"How is my Little Bean doing?" I ask, picking up the picture of Layla and me off the dresser. It's only been a week since I saw her after she was born, but it feels like it's been forever. . I miss all of them. I think if I were around them, I'd feel more grounded.

"She's doing just fine. Mostly eating, sleeping, and pooping." I can hear the smile in Tonya's voice. She is one proud mama. And she deserves all the happiness that comes her way.

"Don't think trying to get me off track by talking about Layla is going to work." Tonya laughs knowing exactly what I was doing. "How did you manage to capture this guy's attention?"

I groan, "I'd really rather not say. It's a long story and I don't really want to get into it." That's only a half truth. I don't want to get into how Travis noticed me, but I also don't want my best friend knowing the dark, self-destructive path I've started down.

I can practically hear the gears turning in my best friend's head. "You're doing okay, right?" She asks. There's worry in her voice. I know I put it there when I was home for Christmas break. She has enough on her plate, though. I don't want to add more to it with my own inner turmoil.

"Absolutely," I lie. I'm pretty sure she can tell I'm not being honest because she sighs on the other end.

"You're lying, but I'll let that drop for now. What does Travis look like? Is he drool-worthy?"

I bark out a laugh. "Yeah, if you think super attractive stalkers are hot." I pause. "He is very easy on the eyes. He's lean but muscular, and he has the bluest freaking eyes I've ever seen. But, he annoys me more than I like looking at him."

Now it's Tonya's turn to giggle. "Girl, you've got it bad. Don't even try to deny it. I don't think I've ever heard you say you want to stare into a guy's eyes. Usually it's more of you want to hook up with them for a little bit of fun."

"I know," I snap. "Sorry, I just wish he didn't think it's his job to save me all the time."

"Save you from what?" Tonya asks. I can imagine her eyebrows furrowing in concern, already trying to figure out a way to help me. Even when she's so far away.

Shit. I've slipped up. What the hell do I say?

My roommate charges through the door at just that moment practically yelling into her phone. "I've gotta go, T. I'll talk to you later." I hang up before she has a chance to respond.

I plop myself on my bed and look over at my roommate, Darcy. She covers her phone with one hand and whispers, "Sorry, it's my grandma."

I grin and shake my head. It's pretty awesome that her grandma calls. I would love for any of my family to call me without feeling the need to bitch about something. The only time I hear from them is when they notice my grades slipping. Then I get long lectures about how I'm not "applying myself." Whatever. I'd probably do better if I was taking classes I actually want to take.

I lie on my bed and stare at the ceiling; while Darcy tries to explain to her grandma how to connect the computer to Wi-Fi. I laugh, it's adorable and hilarious at the same time. I feel a pang in my chest, wishing I had the same relationship with my family.

Finally, she throws her phone on her bed. "I don't understand why she always has to call *me*. Doesn't she realize that my brother lives practically ten minutes from her. He could go over there and do it for her. Instead, I've somehow become her go-to person any time she has technical issues."

Darcy thumps her head against the wall. "Old people should not be allowed to use the internet if they can't figure it out for themselves."

"Look on the bright side," I say. "She must think you are the only person capable of teaching her, or she wants a valid excuse just to talk to you."

She tilts her head to the side. "Huh, I've never thought about it that way. It must mean I'm her favorite." A wicked grin crosses over her face. "I can't wait to tell my brother."

This girl is something else. I was terrified I would have the roommate from hell when I found out that Tonya wasn't joining me at college, but Darcy has become a close second when it comes to best friends. She's been there to hold my hair back more times than I can count. She's never pushed too hard to find out why I tend to get sloppy drunk, and I cherish her even more for that.

Darcy jumps out of her bed. "I almost forgot. That broody guy that was here the other day is downstairs. I was going to wave him up, but that scowl on your face tells me I was correct in not letting him."

"Fuuuck," I groan. "I guess I need to go see what the hell he wants." This better be good, or I may just punch him in his gorgeous face.

travis

THIS DORM REALLY NEEDS to invest in a better heating system. It was cold the last time I came to pester Cami. Though, by the time she finished ripping me a new one, I no longer had a chill.

I'm beginning to wonder if her roommate even told her I was here. It's been fifteen minutes and she still hasn't made an appearance. I know I should probably back off, let her make her mistakes, and deal with the consequences. But I *can't*.

Last semester she was this bubbly personality. Someone you wanted to gravitate toward. I should know. I hung out on the fringes, gathering my courage to ask her out, but never actually went through with it. Winter break came and went. I planned on talking to her when the new semester started up. But she came back different, reckless. Cami always pushed the boundaries a bit. But now, there's not even a glimmer of that carefree soul she had before.

I did end up talking to her, but not in the way I was

hoping. The weekend after classes started, I found her stumbling toward the bathroom at a frat party. It wasn't that her presence at those parties was alarming, she's almost always at them. It was just...the state she was in. It reminded me of too many times in my house growing up. I can't let her do that to herself. It will cause more damage in the future than the pain she's feeling right now, and I know she's hurting. I want to be the one that keeps the pain at bay.

Even with all the thoughts running through my head, I can't help but notice the drabness in this recreation area. I figured with it being a girl's dorm there would be a little more life. Bright colors, something. But it feels sterile. The posters hanging on the walls are those cheesy motivational ones that you usually find in a high school counselor's office. There's a small TV in the corner, but nothing else. There aren't any games, or signs of life. It's giving me a creepy vibe. My dorm hall is better than this. We at least have a pool table and a big television with video games stacked beside it. No wonder she's always in a foul mood. I would be too if this is what I had to walk down to every morning.

I sit up a little, trying to find a somewhat comfortable position in this lumpy couch, when Cami stomps into the common area. She does *not* look happy to see me. The scowl turning her mouth down, and the fire in her eyes is more than evident as she approaches me.

"Why the hell are you here?" She demands, crossing her arms over her chest. Showing her cleavage as she does it.

It's difficult not to let my eyes wander for too long,

but I manage to keep my attention on her face. I'm not one of those smarmy bastards that has to ogle a woman's body any time the opportunity presents itself.

I stand, "I was stopping by to see if you were going to be around this weekend."

She shifts her stance, throwing her hands on her hips. "And, why in God's name would that be any of your business? You are *not* my keeper. I don't know how many times I have to keep telling you this." She's all but yelling now.

I shove my hands in my pockets and smirk. "I never said it was any of my business. I was just wondering if you're busy."

I can tell my casual stance is catching her off guard. Calm and cool, that's me. Well, that's the me I want to portray right now. Inside, my nerves are strung so tight it's a wonder she can't see my hands trembling even though they are safely hidden in my pockets.

When she doesn't say anything, I continue, "Go to dinner with me this weekend."

That gets a reaction out of her. She stares at me, slack-jawed. Mouth moving like she wants to fling obscenities at me, but nothing comes out. I give her a few more minutes to process what I've said. She's used to me just showing up. Maybe, just maybe, if I make an effort to ask her out she won't see me as an enemy. I want to help her, save her. And not just because I like her. I don't want her to go down the same road my mom traveled. It's defi-nitely not a pretty route.

Finally, Cami speaks, "No." It sounds final, like she's not even going to give me a chance.

"What if it's not a date? What if we just go hang out somewhere?" I hope she can't hear the desperation seeping into my words.

"How in the world are you going to make it not a date?" She asks, completely oblivious to my inner anxiety.

"Um," I stammer. "We can hang out in a group setting, go bowling or something." Bowling? Who the hell would think that's a good idea? But I'm grasping for straws, trying to find an activity that will soothe her worry. That will make her consider spending any kind of time with me. I know I haven't exactly caused her to have warm feelings for me. Not when I randomly show up wherever she is. Not when I practically kicked the door down and found her unconscious. But someone has to look out for her, and that someone is me.

She's standing in the middle of the commons area, nose scrunched up, brows dipped down, like she doesn't know how to respond to my last request. The fact that she hasn't shot me down is a positive in my eyes.

"Y-yeah," she stutters. "That might be doable. But, only if Darcy can tag along. I want to make sure this whole thing stays as non-date as possible."

"Who?" I ask.

"Darcy, my roommate," Cami rolls her eyes. The fight is back in her eyes.

She can see the confusion clearing on my face. "Ding, ding. Winner. You know the girl, you tried to let you come up to our room to see me."

"Oh, yeah." I say. "I know who you're talking about."

I knew her name started with a "D", but I couldn't remember it.

She snorts. And sees right through me.

"So, Friday night?" I ask.

"Sure," Cami replies, bored. "I'll meet you at Hilltown Bowling Alley around seven."

Like there's another bowling alley in this town. It may be the home of Hilltown University, but it's still small compared to other college towns. "Great. It's a date."

That was the wrong thing to say. "I mean, I'll see you there."

I don't give her time to say anything about the date comment. I hurry out the dorms front door in the cool February air, and hope like hell she didn't see it as cowardice. I have a date that's not a date to plan in two days, and I need to make it perfect.

I don't hesitate calling Derrick, my friend from back home. He's the only person I can think of to help figure out this whole date thing.

He answers after the first ring, "What's up?"

"Didn't your mom ever teach you the correct way to answer the phone." I laugh.

"Nope." He pauses, "It's been a while. Is everything okay?"

I can only guess that he thinks this has something to do with my mom. We've been friends since we were in kindergarten. His parents would let me come over any time I wanted to escape the confines of my own personal hell. They knew what the situation was at my house, but they didn't know what they could do to make things better for me. They helped more than they will ever know. Derrick's family kept me sane, and out of trouble.

"Helloooo, earth to Travis," I hear over the receiver.

"Sorry," I say. "I was stuck in my head."

"So, does this have to do with your mom?" He questions, cautiously.

"Actually, no," I reply trying to keep the wind out of my ear as I'm walking back to my own dorm. "I need help with a date. Well, a non-date."

"What the hell is a non-date?"

"It's where I'm trying to get this girl to go on a date with me, but she insists on bringing her friend so that it won't be an actual date." I snap.

"That sounds complicated."

"It is, you don't even know the half of it." I take a breath, "So what exactly do I do? We're going bowling."

He laughs, "That's the most unromantic thing in the world."

"She picked it."

"Obviously." I can hear his chair squeaking in the background. He must be playing video games. "There's not much you can do. Just be your charming self, and have fun."

"Easy for you to say," I reply. "This girl makes it impossible for me to think straight around her."

"Don't try too hard. If you have to put in a ton of effort, she isn't worth it."

"Thanks for all the help you didn't give me," I chuckle. "I'll talk to you later. Wish me luck, man."

"Good luck, and remember, be yourself, you've got this." I hear the click of him hanging up before I even have a chance to say anything else.

I guess I'm on my own for this one. Hopefully it won't be too horrible, and I don't screw it up.

cami

I'M in a daze as I take the stairs back up to my room. I could have taken the elevator. I probably would have under normal circumstances, but I need time to process. What in the hell did I just agree to? Only minutes after complaining to Tonya about how much Travis annoys me.

Standing outside my room, I attempt taking a deep, cleansing breath. Hoping it calms my rattled nerves. Sadly, it doesn't. I can see my fingers shaking as I reach for the doorknob. Feel my breath going ragged as I step through the door and rush straight to my nightstand.

I yank my anxiety pills out of the drawer and fumble with the lid before *finally* getting the bottle open. Dropping two small, white ovals in my hand, I turn to the mini-fridge and grab a water. Gulping the medicine and the entire contents of the water bottle in one go. I know I may seem calm and collected, but I'm not. Inside, I'm a jumble of knots, freaking out over giving Travis that little bit of control by agreeing to this non-date.

Pulling the covers back I climb into the corner on my tiny dorm bed. I drag the blankets over me to try to calm the storm raging in my brain. I know to most people this wouldn't be a big deal. A cute guy asked me out *and* is willing to let my friend come. What girl in her right mind wouldn't want that? But my trembling hands are proof that this is too much. I like to be the one in control of situations. It's the one thing I *can* do since my father dictates every other part of my life. It's also the reason I've never really had a boyfriend. I'm not a fan of giving anyone else any kind of hold over my emotions. I'm more of a love 'em and leave 'em type of person, much to Tonya's chagrin.

I wonder if I would be different if I didn't have to walk the straight and narrow for my father all these years. If I was able to choose my own future, and pursue my own passions. Over Christmas break, Tonya told me I needed to do that. I need to chase my own dreams, regardless of what my father says or thinks. But she doesn't understand, she has supportive parents. If I would have gone to mine telling them I was pregnant at eighteen, they would have gone ballistic and disowned me. They also bankroll my tuition. So, I feel like I have to do what they tell me. I'm practically a walking contradiction.

I'm so deep in my thoughts I don't feel the bed dip beside me. The covers are being pulled off me, and Darcy is sitting there staring at me, with a frown marring her face. I already have Tonya concerned about me, I don't need Darcy to share this burden. She doesn't say anything. But she lies down beside me and wraps me in her arms. I've never been a touchy-feely type of person, but this feels perfect. To have someone to lean on when my best friend can't be here.

After a few moments, I throw the blanket off the both of us and take a glance around our dorm room. Darcy and I are two completely different people. She's fun, bubbly, and light. Everything I want to be one day. Everything I used to be before I let my parents control my life.

Her walls are filled with bright colors. From the shelving and containers she has placed around her desk to the posters of whatever Pop bands she's listening to at the moment. My side is doom and gloom if I'm being honest. Lots of blacks and grays. There are a few splashes of pink thrown into the mix. Most of the posters decorating my wall include abstract prints with no rhyme or reason. We may be polar opposites, but having her comfort me means more than anything to me.

Darcy lifts her head. "Are you okay," she asks.

Shaking my head I mumble, "Not really. But I will be, eventually."

"Want to tell me what caused your little tailspin?"

"It wasn't anything major," I sigh. "But I might as well because it includes you."

Darcy's eyebrows shoot up. "What do you mean it includes *me*?"

She sits up so quickly I bounce and nearly fall off the bed. These beds are tiny, and don't do well with a lot of movement. The look of horror on her face is priceless. She must think I'm planning something nefarious. That would almost be better than what our actual plans will consist of.

"W-well," I stutter. I pull my knees against my chest and wrap my arms around my leg. "We are going bowling Friday night...with Travis."

I can see the relief pass over her. Her features soften, and a small grin takes the place of the gasping fish look she had going on. "And, why exactly do I have to go?"

Darcy doesn't know about my anxiety issues, or if she does, she doesn't let on that she knows. I drag my palms over my face. "Because," I say. "I can't go alone. He makes me nervous."

There's a flash of worry in her eyes, and I hurry to rectify that. "No, not like he may try something nervous. Like, I feel unbalanced when I'm around him. I don't know if it's because he's decided to become my own personal savior, or because he's so intense. But my heart rate speeds up every time I'm around him. And, I don't want him to think this is a date. Sooooo, I told him that you had to be able to tag along."

I'm not sure what I was expecting, but it wasn't Darcy falling over in a fit of giggles. I scrunch my nose and attempt to push her off my bed. But she's not having it. She grips the side of the bed to keep from going over.

"Do you think it might be possible that you have a crush on him?" She asks with smirk.

"Absolutely *not*," I protest. "I don't even really know the guy. Except that he thinks it's his mission to keep me from having a good time."

"Having a good time, or getting so trashed you don't

remember anything and completely blacking out?" She levels her gaze at me.

Apparently, she has noticed how often I come home a complete mess. I wonder why she hasn't mentioned anything about it if she's as worried as she appears to be. Tonya would have been all over my ass about it if she were here. That's one thing she's never stood for, and I got my fair share of lectures from her in high school. Darcy just takes it all day by day. I would love to be that carefree and only have pestering grandparents to worry about.

"Um, both?" It comes out more as a question than a statement. "I can't help it. If I'm going to lose control, I'm going to do it on my own terms."

"Why do you need to lose control?" Darcy has scooted closer to me and I didn't even realize it.

I'm not ready to have this conversation. I don't want her to know just how fucked up her roommate has become. I wasn't like this last semester. I was able to go out and have fun without getting drunk off my ass. But my dad's new rules for this semester and the bitchfest I got over break has me struggling to give a damn anymore.

Evasion is always my best tactic. I bounce up on my knees. "So, will you pleeeease go with me Friday night?" I whine.

Knowing she's lost the battle, at least this time, she nods. "Yes, I'll go with you. But don't make things weird." She must sense that I'm about to argue. "And that means no fighting with Travis for no reason. No yelling at him, and please try to keep things civil. There aren't many places to go out in this town, and I don't want to be banned from the bowling alley."

The grin that takes over my face would rival the cheshire cat. "You are the fucking best. I'm so glad I got you as my roomie."

"Yeah, yeah," Darcy pushes me on my butt. "You owe me, lady. I won't tell you what, or when, but you'll be my bitch when I come calling."

She's about to walk out of the room so I grab one of my many pillows and throw it at her. My aim sucks. It hits the wall about three feet from her head. She smirks and leaves me to my own devices.

travis

MY PALMS ARE SWEATING, and it seems like no matter how much I wipe them on my pants, the dampness is there to stay. I don't understand why I'm so nervous. I've been practically trailing Cami for the past couple of weeks just to make sure she doesn't go off the deep end.

Honestly, I'm more scared that she's going to stand me up. I know I told her it wasn't a date, but I want it to be. Even with whatever she's dealing with, I want her. There isn't anything she could do that would make that untrue. It's already 7:20, and she's still not here.

I look like a complete loser, hanging out by the doors of the bowling alley entrance. I can hear the pop music blaring from the speakers in the ceiling. The neon lights are flashing at a rate that's starting to give me a headache. How does anyone bowl a decent game with all these distractions? Maybe I should cut my losses, and just head back to my room. I could see what parties are happening tonight, but I'm not really in the mood for that right now.

I'm pushing the door open, about to step out into the cold February night, when I spot Cami and Darcy walking toward the building. I quickly shuffle back inside. I don't want to seem too eager, even though I am. Desperation isn't a good look on anybody. That's what I am right now. Desperate for any attention she might give me. Even if it's annoyance, I'll take it.

I'm standing by the shoe rental counter when they hurry through the door. Cami is completely bundled up. It's not *that* cold outside, but she's obviously not a fan of the chill. She's unwrapping the scarf from around her neck before peeling her coat off her body. From here, she looks like a terrified bunny; eyes round, lips pressed together, and head shifting left to right as if she's on the lookout for a predator. I'm pretty sure I'm the predator that has her so skittish.

I wave my hand just as Darcy is looking my way. She points to me while murmuring something to Cami. Darcy grabs Cami's arm as if she's keeping her rooted to the spot. If I was a betting man, I would put my money on her bolting. I can tell by the way she's shifted one foot toward the door. She could probably sprint out of here before I have a chance to even greet her. Luckily, Darcy seems to be keeping her in place.

I walk toward them, slowly. I don't want to spook Cami even more than she already is. I can't let this night go down the drain. I want her to open up and see me as more than a nuisance. I wish I knew what was going on inside her head. She doesn't seem to let many people in, not even Darcy.

I come to a stop, two feet in front of them and hold out two flower arrangements awkwardly. I don't know why I picked them up. It just seemed like the right thing to do. At least that's what I gathered from other guys and movies. I didn't exactly have the best relationship role model growing up. Hell, I was lucky if I even met any of the losers my mom paraded through the house.

Darcy's mouth is curved up in a smile. The flowers must impress her. "I thought this wasn't a date?" she asks.

"It's not," I blurt out. "I figured it would be a nice gesture with this crappy, cold weather we're having. Something to brighten y'all's day."

Cami is looking down, but I feel like she may be hiding a grin. Darcy nudgers her with her elbow. When she doesn't say anything, Darcy speaks. "Thank you, they're beautiful."

I shrug. I'm not exactly sure what I'm supposed to say now. An awkward silence fills our area. I don't know what to do. Most people think I'm this really confident guy, and can take charge of any situation, but Cami brings out this deafening insecurity in me.

"So," I say, shoving my hands in my pocket. "Y'all want to bowl?"

"Yes," Darcy exclaims. "It's better than standing here with our heads up our asses."

I burst out laughing. "True enough. Let's go, then."

Cami starts to walk ahead of me, but thinks better of it

and slides back to Darcy's side. This is so unlike how she's acted in the past. I've seen her reserved, but not to this extent. It's almost as if she doesn't trust herself around me. I don't know if I should take that as a compliment or an insult. Maybe she doesn't dislike me as much as she claims. It's definitely food for thought. I just hope she loosens up at some point. I don't know how to navigate the waters with the Cami standing behind me; meek, quiet, and terrified.

We pause at the counter to rent our shoes and lane. I really wish I would have thought of another place to do this whole non-date thing. There's nothing appealing about the smell of feet. And in this small area, the stench is overwhelming. Do they even clean these shoes properly? I'm turning around, about to suggest to the girls that we go do something else, when one of the employees behind the counter clears their throat.

I know that annoyed sound anywhere. It's Erika. She does not seem to be amused with the fact that I'm here with someone else. Wait, when did she get a job here? I've known her since the beginning of last semester. Even when I dated her, she never mentioned having a job.

"What are you doing here...with *her*?" She asks, voice full of venom.

"We're hanging out, not that it's any of your business," I shoot back. I don't have the energy or patience to deal with her bullshit. There's a reason I ended things with her. And most of it is because of her crappy attitude.

She starts to speak up when another employee, Randy according to his name tag, walks up. "Is everything okay over here?"

I snort, "Just peachy."

"Erika, why don't you take a break, I'll take care of them." Randy moves in front of her, not giving her a chance to argue.

"Thanks, man," I mumble. "I don't want any drama tonight."

"No problem," Randy smacks the counter. "Anything to keep our customers happy and comfortable."

"Can we get a lane for an hour and 3 pairs of shoes," I ask.

"Absolutely. That'll be $32.48." Randall answers.

Cami starts to reach for her money, but I quickly stuff some cash in Randall's hand. "Keep the change."

"What shoe sizes do you need?" We rattle off our sizes, and make our way to lane thirteen. I don't know if I should take that as an omen for how the night is going to play out. I'm not superstitious or anything, but Erika's appearance and the way Cami is acting aren't exactly stellar points for this evening.

I grab a couple of balls from the shelf while Cami and Darcy get their shoes on. When I get back to the lane, Darcy is putting names into the computer. I glance up at the screen, and have to take a second look. The names on the screen are enough to make anyone laugh because they aren't actually our names; "Awesome D," "Hot Guy," and "Deb Downer." I didn't know Darcy before, but she definitely has a sense of humor, and I hope some of her enthusiasm rubs off on Cami.

Cami, on the other hand, is sitting on the bench, wringing her hands. I want to know why this makes her nervous. I haven't done anything to make her feel that way. At least, I don't think I have. Finally, she glances up at the screen with our names. I don't know if it's because she heard my laugh, or because she's done zoning out, but she shrieks at Darcy.

"I know 'Deb Downer' is not supposed to be me," she screams.

Darcy just giggles. "Well, you could have fooled me. I'll change it, but *only* if you turn that frown upside down and have fun tonight."

Cami is standing with her arms folded across her chest with a scowl crossing her pretty face. "I'm not frowning."

"That, right there," Darcy says, circling her fingers in the vicinity of Cami's face, "is a frown of epic proportions. So... until that ugly look disappears, you will be known as Deb Downer."

"Ugh," Cami moans. "Why did I ask you to come again?"

"Because you're a chicken shit, and didn't want to be around buddy boy here alone." Darcy waves her hands toward me.

"Maybe I should just...step over here until y'all are finished with your talking," I say, feeling uncomfortable now that the attention has shifted to me.

"Let's just get this game started," Cami sighs. "I'm ready to kick some ass."

I scoff, "I think you've got that wrong. It's me that is going to be doing the ass-kicking."

"It's on, stalker boy," she smirks.

During the first game, we all suck. I like to think of that round as a warm up. We're getting into our groove and figuring out what works best. The second game is a little more intense. I make a few strikes, and Cami does her best to knock me off the top spot. Darcy is goofing off, getting a kick out of the competitiveness bowling has brought out in us.

I win by twenty points. Cami stomps around the lane, showing just how peeved she is by this turn of events. I sit down on one of the hard, plastic chairs and take a sip of my soda. KISS is blaring through the speakers. One of the older employees must have hijacked the music. I don't really want this night to end, yet. The more we've bowled, the more Cami has let her guard down. We've been smack talking and ribbing each other for the past 30 minutes, and our hour is almost up.

While Cami is complaining to Darcy that she should have won, I rush over to the counter. Luckily Randall is still the person behind it.

"Hey, Randy," I say. "I know our time is almost up, and it looks like there's a waitlist, but is there any chance I can pay for one more game."

He looks at the list of names, debating whether he should grant me this request. I can tell he's about to say no.

"I'm trying to impress this girl. I really like her, and I want to make a good impression."

That's not entirely true. I'm trying to impress her, but I'm also hoping I can get her to go out with me again.

"Sure, kid," he says. "Just make it quick."

"Thank you," I yell, already running back to our lane.

Cami is about to take off her shoes, when I stop her. "We're good for one more game. But let's make it interesting."

She quirks an eyebrow. "What do you mean 'interesting?'"

"If I win," I begin, "you agree to go out on an actual date with me."

She starts to argue but I stop her. "If you win, I'll back off."

She brings her finger to the corner of her mouth, contemplating the offer like some sort of evil villain. "Okay, you're on."

I turn to ask Darcy if she's still playing, but she's already removed her name from the list of bowlers. "I want no part of the crazy train that's about to happen."

The first few frames are close. We're pin for pin. I'm starting to pull ahead, but she starts playing dirty. She sways her hips as she lines up for her next shot. Tosses her hair over her shoulder, turns back and winks at me. I mean, who actually does that?

I'm on my last frame, about to roll my ball down the alley, when I see her saunter over to the lane next to me. At some point she pulled her sweater down lower because when she bends to tie her shoelaces, her cleavage is all but spilling out of her top. It's almost as if she's trying to make sure I notice her. I lose my concentration, drop the ball, and it rolls straight into the gutter.

She just kicked my ass using her body. Evil woman. And I've just lost my chance at an actual date with her. I told her I'd back off, but I didn't say how long.

cami

IT'S ONLY BEEN a few days since the epic bowling battle, but I'm still walking on cloud nine after kicking Travis's ass. I figured he would be much harder to defeat, but a little cleavage goes a long way when it comes to most college guys. It definitely proved to be the same for him. All I had to do was bend over. And BAM, the game was mine. I don't think I've ever won anything in my life so easily.

Darcy keeps making fun of me because I'm still wearing my victory smile. Maybe it's a little much, but that win gave me some peace from his constant nagging. Now, though, I kind of miss him following me around. Making sure I'm not getting into trouble. Who is going to be my conscience now? We all know that I'm not very good at doing that myself.

I'm walking out of my accounting class, bleh, when I sense someone behind me. The fact that I *know* it's Travis doesn't mean anything at all. It doesn't mean that I've somehow become attuned to him over the past few weeks.

I keep walking. Head held high as if I don't realize he's literally right behind me. Calling my name.

"Cami," he calls. "Wait up."

Walking a few more feet, I finally turn around, acknowledging he exists. "Oh, Travis," I exclaim. "I didn't even see you there."

"I've been calling your name for the past minute, or so," he grumbles.

My inner bitch is giggling with delight. "Sorry, I must have zoned out. What's up?"

"Would you go out to dinner with me?" he asks.

"I thought me winning the bowling game meant you wouldn't be bugging me anymore," I laugh.

"I believe I said I would back off," he replies. "But, I didn't say for how long."

I groan. Of course he would leave that little tidbit off. I thought everything was going to be golden after last weekend. I liked hanging out with him, but dating him would be an enormous mistake. I don't get serious with guys. I haven't in the past few years. Not since my father yanked all my control from me. I don't want to give anyone else that sort of power over me.

"Look," I start. "Last weekend was fun. I actually had a great time bowling, and kicking your ass. But...the answer is still no. It wouldn't be a good idea. I don't do relationships."

"Just once," Travis argues. "An actual date. No more of this non-date stuff with Darcy tagging along. I promise to take whatever happens slow."

"I said no, Travis. I can't do this right now. Or ever." I storm down the sidewalk. I can't deal with this. Why can't he get a clue? How many times do I have to turn him down before he stops?

By the time I make it to my building, I'm fuming. I don't understand guys. I don't know why they can't grasp the fact that a person may not want to date them. Or, be continuously hounded by them. The hounding part, that's why I am the way I am. My father decided that I would be one to take over his accounting firm. He decided that I would go to college to get a degree in accounting. And, he said if he's paying for it, then I have to major in what he tells me to.

I don't want to do this. I hate anything that has to do with math. It's not where my passion lies. I'd rather be working on clothing designs. I have a sketchbook full of them. They stay hidden under my bed because God forbid my dad find them. I'll get another lecture about how it's a waste of time. And how I will never make a solid living on it. Way to kill my dreams, Pops.

I stop at the elevator, trying to decide if I want to wait on the ancient thing to make its way down or just take the stairs. In the end, I take the stairs. I need to move. I need to do something with this sudden pent up aggression.

I run up the steps, as fast as I can, barely registering the weight of my bag as I sprint toward the fifth floor. By the time I get to my room, I'm gasping for breath. My chest is heaving and I can feel an ache in my side. Maybe I should up my cardio. If this was the zombie apocalypse, I'd easily be food.

I throw the door open as soon as it's unlocked. I search around for Darcy, except she's not here. Why isn't she here? We get out of class at the same time, and she always comes back to the room right after. Wait...what day is it?

I walk over to the dry-erase calendar Darcy mounted to the wall between our desks. Shit, it's Wednesday. Half the week flew by, and I didn't even realize it. She has another class right after chemistry. Who am I supposed to vent to now?

I don't want to call Tonya. I'm sure she's busy being a mom and everything that entails. I can't keep relying on her to bring me down every time I have an attack. It's not fair to her, and I've been a pretty shitty friend lately. I told her I'd stop avoiding her texts and calls when I saw her at Christmas, and again when I saw her a couple of weeks ago, but I'm a mess right now. She doesn't need that in her life. I don't want to bring her down when things are going great with her. She has a family now, and drama is the last thing that needs to occupy her time.

I don't want to rely on medicine to keep pulling me out of the darkness, but I can't think of another way to see the light at the end of the tunnel. I open the drawer of my nightstand, pour a couple of pills in my hand, and slam the drawer shut. The lamp and bottle of water teeter on the surface from the force. I grab the bottle, take a swig and pop the pills that will take me to a happy place.

The wait for Darcy to get home is going to be long and boring. What am I supposed to do for two whole hours? I could sketch a few designs, but nothing would turn out the way it should. It would be tainted by my mood, and I don't want that to come across. I dig in my bag, and pull out my laptop. If I have to wait I might as well be productive.

I'm halfway into my essay on the symbolism in *Beowulf,* for my English class, when my phone rings. I have a half second of excitement thinking maybe it's Tonya, when I look at the screen and "Evil Overlord" is staring back at me. I swear, if he ever saw what I have him listed as on my phone, I'd be cut off for life.

I pick up the phone, wishing I could decline the call, and hit the little green icon. "Hi, Dad."

"Cami," he grunts. The amazing Benjamin Alexander, everyone. Man of many words. More like man of few words unless he's calling to bitch me out. I have a niggling feeling in my gut that a gripe-fest is about to happen.

"How have you been?" I ask, politely. Being rude doesn't get you far with him.

"I'm good, but that's not why I called," he replies.

"What's up?" I question, shutting my laptop so I can be focused on whatever he's about to spew. I know it won't be anything good.

"Your grades are slipping," his says, voice clipped. I can practically see the frown marring his face.

"We haven't had any grades posted, yet. How do you even know that?" I challenge.

I hear him shuffling around, probably putting his phone between his ear and shoulder. "I emailed all of your instructors at the beginning of the semester with a request to let me know if your grades start to fall. I'm upset to see that your grade in accounting has gone down considerably."

"You did *what?*" I screech. "Is that even legal? Why are you checking up on me? I'm doing what you asked. I'm working on my accounting degree, turning all my work in, staying in the dorms when I'd rather have an apartment. What else do you want from me?"

"Listen here, young lady," Dad demands. "I'm paying for your education, and I expect you to keep an A average. Right now, you're not doing that. If I have to go behind your back to find out what is going on, then I will."

I want so badly to hang up on him, but I know that will get me nowhere. He'll just call back and lecture me more. I should have kept my mouth shut, listened to what he had to say, and then agreed to do extra credit or whatever I needed to do to keep him happy. But I can't. I can't keep letting him control my life. Next thing you know he'll be telling me whom to marry, and how many children to have.

"That is beyond not normal, Father." I reply, knowing that he hates when I call him that. "And also, intrusive. I'm doing the best I can. That class does not come easy to me."

"You'd probably do better if you didn't show up to your Monday classes hungover," he retorts. "Your professor told me that, as well. What has gotten into you? If you don't straighten up, I'm going to pull all my funds from your education. No school, no phone...nothing."

I don't even wait to hear what else he has to say. I hang up. That was the last straw. Where the hell does my fucking accounting professor get off telling my father about my actions? It's none of their business.

The anxiety that had finally receded is back in full force. I can't take another dose of my medication, so I do what anybody worthy of a princess performance would do. I throw myself on my bed, sobbing, trying to figure out what the hell I'm going to do.

* * *

My body is being shaken. I must have fallen asleep during my crying fit. I glance over my shoulder, taking in the darkening sky, wondering what time it is.

Darcy whispers, "Wake up sleeping beauty."

"Ugh," I moan. "Why do I need to get up? It's practically bedtime already."

"Girl, it's barely after five," Darcy exclaims. "Why are you asleep anyway?"

I grab my phone checking the time. There are a ton of missed calls from my father and texts from my mother. "I was really hoping everything that happened today was just a dream."

"Bad day, huh?"

"That doesn't even begin to cover it," I mutter into my pillow. "Let's just say I could use a drink, or ten, right now."

Darcy pushes me to scoot over, and plops onto the bed right beside me. "Want to talk about it?"

"Yeah, I think I do."

I feel her fingers comb through my hair. The gesture so soothing, I just might drift back to sleep.

"It all started with Travis," I say.

I can practically hear Darcy roll her eyes. "Why am I not surprised? What happened?"

Rolling onto my back, I stare at the ceiling. I feel ridiculous even complaining about this. In the grand scheme of life, this isn't even a tiny blip on the radar.

"He followed me after class, and asked me on a date. I told him no, and when he persisted, I may have gotten a tiny bit bitchy with him."

"Why?" She gasps. "You had a great time Friday night." Tapping her fingers on her chin, she pauses. "Hell, you didn't even go out and party Saturday night. Which is completely unlike you lately."

"I know," I exclaim. "Friday night was great, and floating on the win high was phenomenal, but you've seen me at parties. You know me pretty well. I don't do relationships."

"I know, I know. But surely you could go on an actual date with the poor guy. He was a perfect gentleman. Why is it such a bad idea?" She questions. I feel like I'm in the middle of an interrogation, or under a psychological evaluation, which might not be a bad idea.

"Would you believe me if I said I have 'daddy issues'?"

Snorting, she says, "Actually, yes. It would definitely explain a lot."

"What's that supposed to mean?" I snap.

Darcy puts her hands up in the air like she's trying to ward me off from physically attacking her. "Don't get your panties in a twist. It's just that when you came back from Christmas break, you started partying a lot harder than you used to. That, right there, screams parental problems."

"You're right," I sigh. "That brings us to the next issue." I pause for dramatic effect, knowing that she'll likely have the same reaction I did to what I'm about to tell her.

"My asshole of a father has an arrangement with my professors. They are supposed to email him any time my grades start slipping. And...one of them told him I came to class hungover,"

Darcy jumps off the bed. I'll be surprised if whoever is below us doesn't complain about the loud noise when her feet hit the ground. "He did WHAT!"

"You heard me." Sitting up, I lift my arms over my head to stretch them out, and roll my neck a few times to work the kinks out of my muscles. "He's keeping fucking tabs on me like I'm some kind of preschooler."

"What are you going to do about it?"

"Honestly, I don't know. I hung up on him when he threatened to cut me off. And this is how you found me." I shrug. "I need to figure something out because this isn't working. I hate my major, I don't want to work for my father's firm, and I feel like I'm losing myself."

"You'll do whatever you have to do. I'm here for you, no matter what you decide."

I think our conversation is over, but she pulls out the whammy. "So what does your dad have to do with not dating Travis?"

"I just told you how much my father controls my

every move. I *can't* give someone else that kind of control over me. And, that's exactly what will happen."

"You don't know that," she states, walking to her bed. She sits back against the wall. "Maybe he's different from every other jackass you've dated. Maybe...this will be a good thing."

"Doubt it," I say. "And I'm not willing to find out." I lie back down, pull the pillow over my head, and fall back asleep. Not caring if it's way too early to go to bed.

travis

CLASS IS ALMOST OVER. I keep glancing at the door to see if Cami is going to make an appearance. Even when she comes to class hungover, she never misses. I can always count on her being in this boring Economics class.

But today...there is a Cami shaped hole in the seat she usually occupies in the back corner of the classroom. I can't keep myself from looking over my shoulder to see if she's going to magically appear. Maybe she's sick? She seemed fine up until I asked her out yesterday. Am I the reason she's not here?

I consider actually backing off, but we had a great time last weekend. I just wish she could see me as more than the annoying guy that gets in the way of her partying. That's not what I'm trying to do, at all. I just want better for her. She deserves something more than getting shit-faced drunk and losing all control of herself.

I wonder if I should check on her. That wouldn't be weird, would it? Okay, so that might be journeying into stalker territory. I'll see if she's anywhere around tomorrow. Surely she'll be fine by then.

I'm walking to the coffee shop after class. It's not bitter cold like it was last weekend, but there's still a chill in the air. There are only two seasons in Texas, but this is the one I like. Summers are just too damn hot, at least when it's cooler I can add as many clothes as I need. Between May and September, you can't shed enough clothes to stay cooled down. It's like the devil's asshole.

I pull open the door, feel the warm gush of air, and take a deep breath. Inhaling the scent of energy. I have so much homework I need to get done before spring break in a few weeks. I'm going to need the caffeine to keep up my momentum.

My phone rings just as I'm about to place my order. Not looking at the screen, I swipe to answer the call, and immediately groan when I hear the voice on the other end of the receiver.

"Travis," she says, voice shaky. "Are you there?"

"Yes, Mom," sighing, I get out of line, and head back outside. I don't want others hearing any part of my conversations with her. "I'm here."

"How are you? Are classes going okay?"

"I'm good and classes are fine," I placate her. "The college experience is everything I dreamed about and expected."

I'm not sure if she can hear the sarcasm in my words. I'm going to have a ton in student loan debt. I could have stayed home and gotten a job while attending a community college. But, I didn't. I had to get away from there. I had to get away from her. Catherine Morton is hard to deal with when she's sober, even worse when she's high or drunk.

"That's good," my mom replies, and then pauses. "I have a question."

I hold my breath. I know what's coming even if I don't want to admit it. "Is everything okay, Mom?"

"Yes, everything is fine. I was hoping you could loan me some money until my next paycheck." Her voice is high pitched and whiney.

"What happened?" I ask, getting angry about whatever lie she is about to tell me in hopes I'll fund her habits.

"Nothing. I'm just a little short this month, and my lights are about to be turned off."

"How short are you?" I deadpan.

"Five hundred bucks," she responds.

"How in the world are you short that much?" I'm angry. I wish she would take care of herself in ways that don't involve her addictions. "I don't have that kind of money mom. I'm scraping by as it is to make sure I have enough to cover the rest of the semester."

"Well..." she drawls. Here it comes, the lie. "My car broke down, and I had to get it fixed."

"I checked your car before I came back this semester, and everything was fine."

"Well, Son, shit happens." She yells.

"I understand that, but I can't give you that kind of money. How am I supposed to eat and pay for school?"

"That sounds like your problem," she snaps.

Oh hell no. I'm pacing up and down the sidewalk.

Trying to keep my voice down. Passersby are staring at me, no doubt feeling the tension radiating around me.

"I'm not sending you the money," I holler. "You'll have to find another way to keep your lights on. If you would pay your bills instead of your dealers, maybe you wouldn't have this problem. "

I hang up before she even has a chance to respond. I can't keep supporting her. Not when she isn't going to help herself. It pisses me off that she cares more about her next fix than she does about her *child's* well-being. But that's the way it's been for as long as I can remember. I keep hoping one day she'll snap out of it, and be the mom I've needed my entire life. That's not going to happen though, not as long as I give her money every time she calls. It ends now.

I walk a couple of blocks to blow off some steam. I don't want to go back to the coffee shop in the state I'm in. I'm always viewed as the cool-headed, mellow guy. I like being that person. I don't like who I become when I let my mother infiltrate my life.

Finally feeling like I can breathe again, like the weight of my mother's problems aren't crashing down on me, I stroll back to the shop. I order myself a coffee, black. I need the boost without sweetening it up the way I see most people do their drinks. Finding a table in the back so I don't have to interact with anyone, I sit down, pull out my textbooks and try to make a dent in the pile of work I have to get done.

* * *

Friday nights are my favorite night of the week. I can do whatever I want, without having to go to class on Saturday. I need to work on my assignments, but after the conversation with my mom yesterday and Cami's absence, I need to get out of my dorm. I'm one of the lucky few that doesn't have a roommate. He dropped his classes the first week of this semester, and they never moved anyone else in. But it gets lonely.

My mind wanders to Cami. I'm determined to go check on her, but if something was wrong, surely Darcy would mention something. I mean, I'm not her boyfriend or anything, but I think Darcy can see how I feel about Cami.

I throw on a Henley shirt, some jeans, my favorite Doc Martens, and grab a light jacket. I would get my coat, but the parties I'm planning on stopping by tend to stay warm with all the bodies crammed into a tiny space. It would be every zombie horde's dream if the apocalypse ever broke out.

Walking at a brisk pace through the quiet streets of Hilltown, I look at my phone and see all of the texts my mother sent me. I'm not answering them. I told her I wasn't sending the money, and I'm not going to allow her to guilt me into doing it. It blows my mind that she thinks I'm going to support her horrible habits. If she were truly in need, I'd help her at the drop of a hat. But not for this. Not for the lifestyle she continues choosing to live.

I can hear the bass of music as I get closer to the apartments on the outskirts of the university area. I can already tell by the shouts and laughs coming from the complex that it's going to be a crazy night. It's still early, I don't see how they are already as buzzed as they are.

The party is on the second floor, I run up the steps. Dodging people sitting down outside. I really hope nobody calls to complain about the noise. I doubt it though, since this building is primarily college students, but stranger things have happened.

I walk into the living room. The door is wide open so I didn't really see a need to knock. Nobody ever does at these things. People are shouting their "hello's" to me, and I just nod my head. I don't know who half of these people are, and I'm not sure how they know me, but I don't want to be rude. This is the easiest way to greet people without knowing their names.

I grab a solo cup, angle it, and start pouring beer from the keg. I don't usually drink, but stress has me doing all kinds of things I don't normally do. I lean against the kitchen counter, taking in my surroundings. I figured more people I knew would be here, but looks like I'm hanging out by myself tonight.

The smell of weed permeates the air, and it's enough to make me choke. I know the smell anywhere. It stuck to the walls of my house, in my clothes, and the furniture. If Mom wasn't popping pills, or drinking herself into a stupor, she was getting so high she would pass out on the living room sofa. Leaving me to deal with the deadbeat of the night.

I quickly vacate the kitchen. I know I'm not going to be completely free from the festivities happening in here, but I can at least move in the opposite direction of the smokers sitting on the balcony. I round the corner searching for a free space to stand when I bump into Darcy, almost knocking her down.

I throw my hands out to catch her before she falls. "I'm sorry. Are you alright? I didn't see you there."

"Yeah," she says pulling her skirt down, making sure it's not showing anything inappropriate. "I was trying to find someone to help me with Cami, but since you're here, maybe you can."

"Is she okay?" I ask.

"If you want to call it that," Darcy shouts over her shoulder.

I have to walk faster just to keep up with her. We start down the hallway when she comes to a halt in front of a bedroom door. Luckily it's cracked so we can kind of hear what is going on in there. The catcalls coming from multiple people doesn't bode well.

I push Darcy aside, and throw open the door. I can't process what I see without my blood boiling. Cami is standing on top of a coffee table in front of a television. It appears to be some kind of game room, so at least I'm not walking into anything that could land me in jail.

Evanescence is blaring from the surround sound speakers, and Cami is dancing on top of the table. Barely keeping from going over the edge of the small rectangle. She's swaying her hips while dipping low and coming back up again. It looks like she's giving these guys a clothed striptease, and they don't have the decency to stop her when they can tell that she's not sober.

Hell, I can tell she's drunk without her looking at me. Her movements are sloppy and stilting. She is doing her best not to lose her balance in those ridiculous heels she's wearing. Her ass is barely covered by the black mini skirt she's wearing. Finally, she looks my direction, and her eyes are glazed and dilated. I'm hoping she's just drunk and not on something, too.

I turn toward Darcy. "How long has she been like this?"

"About thirty minutes. I came to the party with her to try to keep an eye on her. But when we got here she started taking shot after shot. And I think she took her anxiety medicine before we left the dorm." Her eyes are watery, and she looks like she's about to burst into tears. "I'm such a shitty friend for letting her get like this."

I grab her shoulders to get her attention. "This is not your fault," I say. "You can't control what other people do. Believe me, I learned that lesson a long time ago."

She nods, "Can you get her out of here?"

"Yeah, just give me a second."

I walk all the way into the room, stopping at the edge of the table. When Cami turns she almost falls, and I put my hands out to keep her steady.

"What are you doing here?" she snarls.

"Taking you home." I command in a tone that brooks no arguments.

Except, this version of Cami is confrontational, and she's not having it. "You don't get to tell me what to do. I'm not ready to go."

"You see your friend over there?" I point toward Darcy. "She's worried about you. She ran into me and asked me to help her." I begin pulling her down from the table. "And that's what I'm going to do."

She's fighting me. Kicking, screaming, swinging her

arms trying to hit any part of my body that she can. "I'm not going anywhere with you," she screams.

The guys on the couch start to stand up, but with one glare in their direction, they quickly put their asses right back where they belong. I'm not going to get her out of this apartment with her beating on me. I sling her over my shoulder and carry her out fireman style. She's still pounding on my back and screaming obscenities, but at least she won't give me a black eye.

We walk through the house, Darcy on my heels trying to talk some sense into her friend, and everyone staring at us. When we get to the front porch, I set her down so it's easier to take the stairs to the sidewalk. She's wobbling on her way down, so I grab her waist to steady her. That was the wrong thing to do.

"Why are you even here, Travis? I don't remember asking for your help."

"Well, too damn bad. You're getting it," I argue. "Do you have any idea what could have happened to you up there? What those guys might have done to you?"

"That is for me to worry about," she yells. "You have no right to manhandle me in front a room full of people."

"I do when it's for your own good." I yell back. This night is not going how I hoped it would. I just wanted to relax, have a good time, forget about the stress in my life. This whole scene is the exact opposite of that. And, I obviously worried about her for no reason. She was well enough to come out and get drunk tonight.

She slaps me. Hard. "I don't need you to save me. I can save myself. Why can't you understand that?"

Cami turns around and stomps the rest of the way

down the stairs, practically sprinting down the sidewalk to get away from me.

Darcy pushes in front of me, worry evident by the furrow of her brows, and the way she's biting her lip.

"Can you handle her from here," I ask. "I don't think it's a good idea for me to interfere anymore."

Darcy nods, and runs to catch up with her roommate, without a word.

I may have deserved the slap for the way I carried Cami outside, but I won't apologize for it. Those guys would have waited until she could barely stand, and who knows what would have gone down if I wasn't there.

After about fifteen minutes, I walk back toward campus. I know I said I don't need to be around her, but I *have* to make sure she got back to her room okay. When I'm outside her dorm, I glance up. I see Tonya pacing in front of the window and figure they are good.

When I get back to my room, I plop onto my bed. How did I leave one mess, just like this behind, only to find myself falling for a girl in the same situation?

cami

I AM FURIOUS. Where the hell does Travis get off thinking he can manhandle me like that? I'm wearing the floor of my tiny dorm room thin, trying to wrap my head around what just happened.

Darcy is sitting on her bed, watching me, with a look of horror on her face. "Why did you have to get like that tonight? You said you just wanted to go out and have a little fun."

I stop my pacing, staring out the window. She's against me, too? She's never said anything about how I come home from parties before.

"What's that supposed to mean?" I ask.

"I mean," she starts. "You don't have to get sloppy drunk, and dance on tables, to have a good time."

I think she's done, but she continues. "What would have happened if those guys would have laid hands on you, or tried to do something to you? I'm not very big, I wouldn't have been able to stop them by myself."

I want to lay into her, but she has a point. She's never

been to the parties with me. She doesn't *see* the way I act, or what I do. She only sees the aftermath. If I'm lucky enough to make it home.

"But did you have to get *him* to help? There were so many other people at that party, why did it have to be Travis."

Darcy shifts on her bed, scooting over, to make room for me. "Sit down." She pats the space next to her. "I didn't plan on getting Travis to help me. I was going to find someone when I, literally, bumped into him. He was the first person I saw, so I grabbed him and led him to the room."

She pauses and wraps her arm around my shoulder, pulling me toward her. "I didn't know what else to do. You scared me. I mean, I know you're not a super happy person, but I've never seen you like that. Is that what you do when you go out and come home barely able to walk?"

Her concern breaks my heart. This is why I haven't told Tonya anything. I didn't want to make her worry or scared for me.

I don't have any words. I just nod and push myself closer to her. Darcy, somehow knowing I need a hug, puts her other arm around me, allowing me to find the comfort I need.

These moments are why I miss Tonya. She is my person, the one who knows everything about me. Well, everything except my recent partying tendencies. I wish she were here to help me through all the craziness going through my head. I know she has her own life, and I'm happy for her. She deserves nothing but the best. But a part of me feels like I've lost her.

That thought makes me start crying, hard. I know Darcy can feel my chest heave as I sob over everything, and nothing. Compared to most people, I have it made. My parents are taking care of my college education, even if it's not what I want to do for the rest of my life. I don't have to work, and I have people that care about me, even when I push them away. But my brain goes to these dark places when something happens, it could be something small, and it's hard to come out of it.

I can feel Darcy patting my back with one hand while the other is brushing through my unruly hair, trying to calm me down. I don't deserve her, and I've been a pretty shitty friend, and roommate, to her. I need to make sure she knows how much I appreciate her support, even when I don't deserve it.

Slowly, I pull away from her, wiping the tears from face. I'm trying to compose myself, but it's hard when I'm hiccuping, still catching my breath.

"I'm sorry," I say.

Darcy grabs my hand. "You don't have anything to be sorry about, we all have our moments."

"Not for that," I reply. "For putting you in the position to have to take care of me. And, for lashing out when all you were trying to do was help me."

"It's all good, girl," she says. "That's what friends are for. I know I'm not your best friend, but I'm here for you whenever you need me."

"I know just the thing to show you how much I appreciate you."

* * *

Darcy and I are hanging out at a nail salon. It's the first thing that came to mind to show her my thanks. I haven't had a manicure or pedicure in forever. Spring break is coming up, and what better way to welcome it than a little pampering. Now, if only the weather would cooperate with Spring Break festivities. I plan on going home for the week. I'm having Layla withdrawals, and I want to catch up with Tonya. I need to be upfront with her about all the things that are going on.

I've had her as my only friend for so long, maybe my friendship with Darcy will become just as important to me. Especially, when Tonya is busy killing the mother-hood. I don't think she realizes how much respect I have for her.

"You look deep in thought over there," Darcy says, wincing as the nail technician attacks her feet.

"Just thinking," I mumble. "I really need to be a better friend all the way around." I shift in my chair, causing the lady working on my feet to glare at me. "I think I'm going to call Tonya, and let her know what's been going on with me. But I know she's going to freak out, and try to come down here as soon as we hang up."

"Would that be such a bad thing?" Darcy asks.

"Not really, but her travel also involves an adorable baby and her boyfriend. And Layla is only a few weeks old."

"I see." Darcy replies. She's tapping her chin, eyebrows furrowed like she's deep in thought.

I giggle. Even though I've roomed with Darcy for

54

more than one semester, I didn't realize how funny and goofy she can be. That is what I want for my life. I want to be filled with happiness and feel comfortable with myself. I hate being riddled with so much uncertainty, and all the insecurities I can do nothing about. Always wondering if I'm going to be good enough for my family, and if they would see me as less than perfect if I allowed myself to just be me.

I glance over at Darcy. She's lying in the massage chair making faces as the tech scrubs her feet. "Have you ever thought about being more than *just* my friend, like maybe one of my best friends?"

She breaks out into a huge grin, the elation on her face evident. "Absolutely," she exclaims. "I've just been waiting for you to open up some. I didn't want to force myself on you like some crazy lady."

I smile back. "Alrighty then, we are now BFF's."

Getting comfortable, now that the painful part of the pedicure is over, I ask, "Want to grab some pizza after this?"

She grabs ahold of my hand. "You are shaping up to be the best, best friend ever."

We are walking out of the nail salon, Darcy asking what kind of pizza I want so she can order it from her phone, when my phone chimes with a message. I wait until we get to the car before checking to see who it is. My stomach drops after I read the words.

Mom: *Your father expects you to come home over Spring Break and intern at the office.*

I throw my phone on the seat of my car. What the hell? Can my father not grow a pair and ask me if I want to intern? No, he has to demand it. Apparently since I'm his child he gets to tell me what to do.

"I'm guessing it was bad news," Darcy says.

I don't even bother responding, I just hand her my phone.

"Ugh," she groans. "We're going to need extra everything on our pizzas."

"You can say that again," I mutter. "When we get back to the dorm, I need to start looking at part-time jobs. I don't want to be under my father's thumb any longer."

travis

I'VE SEEN a big change in Cami over the past week. I haven't had the guts to talk to her after carrying her out of that party, but she seems...different. She has a confidence and determination that she didn't have when she came back from Christmas break. Maybe now she won't be so averse to going on a date with me. Or, maybe I should just drop it. She made it clear that she didn't want anything to do with me when she stormed off last weekend.

I'm pulling out my spare set of sheets, getting the other bed in my room ready. Derrick is coming up for Spring Break. I feel like it's been forever since we've hung out, but it's only been a couple of months. I thought about going home for break, but I didn't want to have to deal with my mother. It didn't take much to talk Derrick into coming here.

I think he's excited to see what campus life is like. I know he's ready to move out of his parents' house, though I can't imagine why. He doesn't have to cook, or pay outrageous fees to stay in the dorms. Hell, he doesn't even have to do laundry. I think that's the part I loathe the most. Not because I haven't been doing my own laundry since I was a kid, but because I have to walk down to the basement to wash my clothes every week. It wouldn't be a big deal, but that's five floors I have to go down with a basket, and come back up. I wish I would have been able to pick a room closer to ground level.

I don't even know what we're going to eat while he's here. I don't have a ton of money. I have a little bit left over from my student loans, and I started tutoring to earn extra money. I can't say it's my favorite thing in the world, but I can't turn down the money right now.

There's a knock on the door, and I glance at the clock. It's only two o'clock. Derrick won't be here for another few hours. I throw the jumbled comforter on the bed to see who could be here. I don't get visitors very often, choosing to only hang out with most people at parties.

I'm shocked when I open the door, standing in the hallway is Cami. Looking slightly petrified, like she isn't sure she should be here. She's chewing on her bottom lip, looking at the floor, not registering that the door is in fact open.

Finally, she looks up. "Hi," she mumbles. "Can I come in for a minute?"

"S-sure," I stutter. I can't believe she's in my dorm. I can't believe she sought me out. "How did you know which room I was in?"

She shrugs, "I asked around."

Cami is looking all over my room, no doubt trying to find out more about me. She won't find much. I don't spend a ton of time in here, just to sleep and get homework done, unless I'm playing one of my video games online with Derrick. That happens a lot more than it should considering my full class schedule and tutoring jobs.

She's staring at the TV I have set up on one of the desks. It's nothing big, a hand-me-down from Derrick when he got a new one. His parents gave me a second-hand PlayStation when I left for college as a going away gift. I think they knew I would crave some kind of normalcy and the little piece of home I found at their house.

Cami turns around, abruptly, almost slamming into me. I didn't realize I was so close to her. "I wanted to come by and apologize," she says.

"For what?"

"The way I unleashed on you last weekend," she's looking at her feet again. This whole confrontation must be making her nervous. "I was drunk and acting like an idiot. I know it's not an excuse, but I hope you can forgive me."

"Sure," I reply. I've never had anyone apologize to me. I'm not exactly sure how I'm supposed to react. "What brought on this sudden change of heart?" I ask, immediately regretting the words. I didn't mean to sound like a jerk.

Cami flinches like she's been punched. "I guess I deserve that." Clearing her throat she adds, "I'm trying my best to not be bitter and take control of my life in a positive way. I scared the hell out of Darcy, and I don't want to ever put her in that position again."

"This is definitely a step in the right direction, making amends and all that." I take a step back, not wanting to crowd her when she's already feeling uncomfortable. "Do you want a water or something? I may have some cokes in the fridge."

She shakes her head, "No. Thank you, though. I need to head out. I just wanted to come by and say I was sorry for being a bitch."

She moves toward the door, but I'm not ready for her to leave. Maybe I can get to know more about her when she's calm, and less chaotic. "Are you sure? You don't have to leave yet."

"Yes," Cami grabs the doorknob. "I've got a couple of interviews lined up this afternoon. I need to prepare myself."

"Job interviews?" I question. "Why?"

"Because," she lets out a breath, "I'm tired of living by my father's rules, and the only way that's going to change is if I can provide for myself."

With that, she walks out the door, closing it gently behind her.

* * *

"Dude, watch out," Derrick yells at me. "There's a zombie to your left."

Derrick showed up about an hour ago with a casserole dish in hand. There are a million and one reasons why I love his parents, and kind of wish they would adopt me, even though I'm officially an adult. They are always looking out for me, even when they don't have to.

"I see him," I grumble. "That asshole is fast. Did you put the game on veteran mode?"

The maniacal grin on his face is answer enough. "Seriously, man? You know I'm not as good as I used to be."

"Aw, does someone need me to put it on easy?" He asks. "I figured you needed a little push. When we talked the other day you seemed pissed, and the best way to get out of that funk is to kill zombies." He stretches his arms over his head. "Why were you mad, anyway? You never did tell me."

I groan. I didn't really want to go there tonight, but after today's exchange with Cami, maybe he can give me some advice. He's had more serious girlfriends than I have. "Do you remember that girl I took out on a non-date with her roommate?"

He nods, fingers moving fast killing as many zombies as he can.

"Well," I start, pausing to take care of the dead soldier that popped up on my screen. "I asked her out after that, and she turned me down. Then, last weekend I literally had to carry her out of a party because she was drunk and acting ridiculous in front of a group of guys. Then she slapped me for helping her out of a situation that could have gone really bad."

"Okay," he drawls. "Why don't you leave this chick alone? She sounds like a headache to deal with."

"She came by this afternoon, before you got here."

Derrick pauses the game so that he can give me his full attention.

I set my controller next to me on the bed. "She

wanted to apologize for acting the way she did. I think she's going through something, but I'm not sure what." Grabbing my water from the nightstand I continue, "She seems different, though. I don't know if she had a light-bulb moment, or what, but she seemed sincere. I don't know what to do about her. My brain tells me I should wash my hands of her, but I don't know if I can."

"I see," Derrick says, scratching his chin. "You need to decide if she's worth the trouble. From what you said, she sounds a lot like how your mom gets when she's partying. Is she worth the potential heartbreak?"

"When did you become all psychological?" I ask. "Yes, I think she is. There's a part of her that she keeps hidden. I've seen glimpses of it when she's with her friend, Darcy. I just hope that maybe she'll let me see that part as well. I want her to see me as more than a nuisance with a white knight complex. Yes, I'm aware I have that problem."

"As long as you know that you like to save people." He says, laughing. "But, if you want to give it a shot, I say go for it. I'll be here if it goes badly. Why don't you try taking her out this week while you're on spring break?"

"I don't want to intrude on your time here," I reply. "I'd be a pretty shitty host if I did that."

"Don't worry about me," he says. "If I'm lucky, I'll be coming here next year. I'll use that time to peruse the neighborhood, maybe find a spring fling."

"I'm sure it won't be hard. It's not like you've had trouble picking girls, ever." I roll my eyes.

"That's because I have confidence, my friend," he grins. "Something you need to get a little more of."

"I'm working on it," I mutter.

"Enough with all this sappy girl talk," Derrick declares. "Let's kill some zombies. You definitely need the practice if your health level is any indication."

I don't remember how long we play Call of Duty, but my mind is on how I'm going to ask Cami out without pissing her off.

cami

UGH, what is that horrible noise. I sit up, rubbing my eyes, trying to find the source of loud screeching. It's close, whatever it is. I'm almost tempted to lie back down and ignore it, but I know I won't be able to sleep with that incessant racket.

My mind is starting to wake up a little more when I realize that it's my alarm on my phone. Why in the hell would I set it to that tone? Oh, I know, because it's the only sound that will make me get out of bed. It's not super early, but it's earlier than I usually wake up when I don't have classes.

It's the first day of Spring Break, and I have to get ready for my brand new job. I didn't think I would be able to find one so late in the semester that will work around my class schedule. Darcy told me they just fired a barista for coming to work hungover too many times. She also made me swear that I would never do that because she vouched for me to get this position. I swore on my future first born child, that's how bad I need this job.

I look over at Darcy's bed. She's furrowed in her blankets with the pillow over her head. I guess she's using it to muffle my alarm, though I can't see how she's still sleeping through it. I turn off the offending noise, and stumble around my room trying to gather up everything I'll need for my shower. There's a chance I'll forget something, but right now, I don't really care. At least all the bathing essentials are in the caddy. I pick it up and head to the shower on this level. I really wish they would add a bathroom to each individual room, or even between rooms. It would definitely make early mornings so much easier.

I'm dressed and ready to take on the world. Well, maybe not the world, but the day. I really need to make a good impression, I *need* this job if I'm going to get out from under my father's thumb. Then he can't tell me what my major should be. I know a part-time job isn't going to take care of all my expenses, but it's a start. I plan on spending the rest of my break looking at scholarships and any grants the college may offer. I know it's late in the game. I'll probably have to finish out this semester with the great Benjamin Alexander breathing down my neck. But next year, I'll do it on my own. I'll even get a student loan if I absolutely have to, just to be able to make my own decisions again. I don't do well with being told what to do, even if I should be used to it.

I feel myself going to a dark place again. I need to shun that negativity and focus on putting one foot in front of the other. It's the only way I'm going to turn my life around and become someone I can be proud of. I also just realized that I haven't talked to Tonya in a few weeks. Which also means that she doesn't know I got a job, and I'm not coming home.

It's eight o'clock in the morning, but I have a feeling she'll be awake. I search for her name on my phone, and speed dial her.

"Is everything okay," Tonya asks, alarm in her voice.

"Yeah, why wouldn't it be?"

"Let's see... I haven't talked to you in *weeks*, you usually text, and it's early for you," she responds. I'm pretty sure she's ticking the points off on her fingers. She knows me all too well. If I have a chance to sleep, I'm going to take it.

"Yeah, sorry about that. I've been going through some stuff." I twirl my hair around my finger. It's a nervous habit I picked up in high school when things made me anxious, and I didn't want anyone realizing there was anything wrong with me.

"What kind of stuff," her voice is laced with concern. This is why I haven't told her about my spiral into negativity. I don't want her worrying.

"Nothing important," I say, quickly changing the subject. I don't want to mention anything until I know I'm heading toward a better place in my life. "I just wanted to call and tell you that I'm not coming home for break."

She screeches, "Why the hell not? I've been looking forward to seeing you since you left after Baby Bean was born."

"For a good reason, I promise."

"And what exactly is this good reason?"

"I got a job," I exclaim.

"Really," she asks. "What brought on this need to be an employed adult?"

"I'll give you two guesses, but you'll only need one," I mutter.

"I'm guessing it has to do with that man you call a father," she deadpans.

"You'd be correct. I can't handle all the pressure he puts on me. He demanded I come home for Spring Break and intern at his office. It was the last straw." I shrug, knowing she can't see me, but feeling the need to do it anyway. I happen to be a very animated person when I'm talking. My hands are usually flying everywhere, but there's still a chill in the early March morning, and I'm trying to keep the one not holding the phone warm.

"I'm proud of you," she all but shouts. "It's about time you stood up for yourself when it comes to your parents. I've never understood their need to be so involved in your life."

"Me either." I'm getting close to Roasted. "But hey, I need to let you go. I'm almost to work, I'll let you know how my first day of adulting goes."

"Alright, hon." Tonya says. "Good luck, you've got this. Love you."

"Love you, too" I say right before I end the call.

I pull open the door, the scent of coffee beans almost overwhelming, but giving me the energy boost I need to get through my shift.

I walk around the counter looking for Tom, my boss. My hands start shaking, a sign that a panic attack is coming on. I don't need to start the day off like this. When the attacks come on, I tend to hide from the world. I can't be that Cami today. I have to put on my big girl panties and try to deal with it as best as I can.

Finally, I spot Tom coming out of the small office in the back of the kitchen. I must look like I'm about to pass out because he pauses. "Hi, Cami." He studies me some more. "Are you okay? Do you need to eat something?"

I shake my head, not sure which question I'm responding to. Tom walks to the oven, where a batch of hot muffins is sitting. He grabs one with a pair of tongs, wraps it in a napkin, and hands it to me. "Eat this, you'll feel better."

Tom is an older man, probably old enough to be my dad. "My daughter has anxiety issues, and you look exactly like she does when she's about to freak out."

"Thank you," I mumble through the bite of food I just stuffed in my mouth.

"No problem. If things start to be too much, let me know."

I wipe the crumbs from my lips. "I will."

"Let's start you off with something easy today. How do you feel about working in the kitchen?"

"I'm not a very good cook," I reply, still nibbling on the little piece of heaven in my hands.

"Don't worry about that. You'll mostly be restocking the items in the display beside the counter. Something to ease you into the job."

"That would be great, thank you." I can't express how much it means to me that my boss recognized the signs of my impending panic, and offered a solution to help lessen it.

I'm not a hundred percent sure why the thought of working has me flipping out. But I'm grateful for Tom's kindness. I think this whole job thing may work out. When Darcy comes in for the start of her shift, I think it will be easier as well. She'll help me navigate my way around the shop And, it's really hard to have negative thoughts when she's always so upbeat. Even though Tonya is miles away from me, I'm glad I've found a person close by that will always be in my corner.

travis

I DON'T EVEN KNOW what sleep feels like anymore. Since Derrick has arrived all we've done is play video games until the sun starts to come up. We did manage to go shoot some hoops yesterday. He kicked my ass every single time. I really need to increase my cardio. The only other time we've been out of my room is to grab some fast food, only to return and play more games. I'm going stir crazy. I think this is the most time I've ever spent in here.

I'm barely moving, trying to find a state of wakefulness just to climb out of bed. I can hear Derrick moving the joysticks on the controller already.

"Dude," I mutter, "do you even sleep?"

"I'll sleep when I'm dead," says Derrick. "Now, get your ass out of bed and help me conquer this level."

I groan. I do *not* want to play anymore games. Is it possible to get carpal tunnel from video games? I sure as hell hope not. My wrists and hands feel stiff, and I'm not sure I can even hold the controller. But I'll do this for him. I rarely get to see him since I avoid going home at all costs. I'm determined to make the most of this week.

Just when I'm about to suggest we turn off the game system and do something I hear something hit my dorm window. Pulling back the curtain I glare at the dark gray sky, willing the huge drops of rain to stop falling. There goes any chance of doing something outside. I don't want to be stuck in this room any longer. If I do, I may strangle my best friend. I love him like a brother, but who in the hell spends this much time playing video games?

Derrick presses pause on his controller. "I need to get out of here for bit. Wanna go somewhere?"

"For the love of God," I exclaim, "Yes. I've been waiting for you to stop playing for what seems like forever."

After turning the game off, Derrick joins me by the window. He glances around surveying the landscape, like he's waiting for something to pop out and get him. "Do you think it's cold out there?"

I shrug, "Probably. It's been a little chilly all week. The rain is only going to bring the temperature down more."

"Well, shit," he says. "I didn't bring a hoodie or anything."

I point at the closet door, "I have a few in there, grab you one."

This fool comes out wearing my favorite Cowboys hoodie. He couldn't have picked any of the other ones? He *had* to pick the one he knows I wear all the time. "Dude, really?"

"Yep," he says, caressing the sleeves, ""It's crazy soft and will keep me warm and toasty."

"It's not freezing out there, you know that right?" I question.

"I mostly just want to piss you off," he grins. "Is it working?"

I make my way toward Derrick, nonchalantly, then pull him into a headlock. I let him struggle for a few minutes, until he says "uncle" and I release my grip.

"Where do you want to go?"

"How the hell should I know," he replies. "I'm not from around here."

"Coffee it is," I say. "I need it after the lack of sleep since you've been here. Do you stay up late every night? There's no way I'd be able to function."

He smirks, "That's because I'm made of awesome. I can withstand the tiny hours of sleep unlike you mere mortals."

"Shut up, asshole. You are not normal." I reply.

I grab my keys, wait until Derrick vacates the room, and lock up behind me. Any other day I would walk to Roasted, but I'm not about to get soaking wet, and cold, just to get a little caffeine fix. We walk down to the street where my SUV is parked. It's nothing special, but I worked my ass off for it. It was the first thing I ever bought myself after I turned sixteen. I worked summers and breaks, saving every little penny, just so my mother wouldn't be able to tell me what I could and couldn't do with the vehicle.

I'm lost in my thoughts when I realize we're already at Roasted. It's a good thing I know how to get here with my eyes closed. I don't even remember driving here. That's what happens when I think about my past, and my mother.

You would think parking would be more available on a rainy day like this. Nope, I can't see a single space open in front of the shop. What is it about bad weather that brings people out in droves? Had I not *needed* to get out of that tiny dorm, I'd be happily sitting my ass on my bed watching TV or something. Anything to avoid the rain.

Finally, I spot a car pulling out of a space right in front of the door. I look both ways, checking to make sure I won't hit anyone, and whip into the tiny spot. It's made for cars, but I do my best to squeeze into it. As long as another big vehicle doesn't try to park next to me, we're good.

As soon as I open the door, and hear the tiny ding, I feel an awareness. One I only get when I'm around a certain someone. Don't ask me how I'm so attuned to her presence, but I am. I look around the small shop, trying to spot her at a table. Except, she's not sitting at any of them. Maybe it was just wishful thinking. Hoping she would be here so I can finally ask her on a real date, and not have her stomp off and act like a crazy person.

I'm still looking behind me, trying to see if maybe I missed her, when I hear her voice coming from behind the coffee counter.

"Welcome to Roasted, how can I help you today?" She asks with a friendly smile on her face. A smile I've only seen once, when she kicked my ass in bowling.

I turn around with a huge smile on my face, making sure my dimples are showing. If I've learned anything it's that girls love dimples, or so I've been told. The minute she realizes it's me, her mouth drops open, eyes go wide, and cheeks blush a bright pink. Why is she embarrassed?

"Tr-Travis," Cami stutters. "Wh-what are you doing here?"

"Getting coffee, just like everyone else, Beautiful," I reply with a smug smirk. "What are you doing here?"

"I work here," she rolls her eyes, "Obviously."

"Yeah, obviously," I set my hands on the counter, leaning forward just a bit. I don't want to crowd her, but I also don't want her to think I've lost interest.

"Mmhmm," Derrick clears his throat behind me. "Care to introduce me to your friend?"

He's already getting his charm ready. He steps beside me, one elbow on the counter, his other hand in his pocket, managing to look like he's not trying even when he is.

I step back, just a little. "Cami, this is Derrick. Derrick, this is Cami."

"So you're the one Travis keeps going on about," Derrick says with a wink.

Ugh, why did he have to mention that. Is he trying to make me look lame? Now I'm the one blushing. I duck my head, hoping she doesn't notice that I'm getting red. I don't think it works because when I peek up at her, she's grinning. But, it's not a maniacal grin like she's given me before. It's sweet and genuine. I decide, right then and there, that's my favorite expression on her. It's unguarded, and not weighed down by whatever she's been going through.

Cami is full on smiling now, and maybe I was wrong, this is my favorite smile. "So, you talk about me a lot?"

"I might have mentioned you once or twice," I shrug. Then I run my hand through my hair because I don't know what to do. I feel awkward now, like she found out a secret, and has the ability to crush me with it.

"I'm sure." She gets closer to the register. "So, what can I get y'all? I'd love to sit and chat all day, but I do have a job to do."

Derrick gives his ridiculously complex coffee order as Cami puts it into the computer. I'm surprised she can remember anything he said since he was talking so fast. Hell, I can't even remember and this isn't the first time I've heard him order it.

"What about you Travis?" she asks. "Do you like your coffee as fancy as Derrick's?"

I laugh. I'm not used to this version of Cami. She's playful, flirty, and gives Derrick crap about his coffee tastes. That's a mark in the pro column for her.

"Nope," I say, popping the 'p,' "Just black. I'll add the sugar over at the station."

"Hmm, I didn't take you for a strong coffee guy," she says, putting her hand on her hip.

"There is one more thing I'd like." I say, taking up the same stance Derrick did earlier. If it works for him, maybe it'll work for me.

Cami leans forward in anticipation, "What's that?"

"A date." I reply matter of fact.

"A date?" she asks, brows scrunched together.

Is she really that shocked? I've been attempting to

flirt with her since I realized she was the one behind the counter.

Derrick has already moved on to the other end of counter, studying everyone. Most likely picking out his spring fling conquest. A woman behind me starts tapping her foot, annoyance written all over her face.

Cami blows out a breath, either on the verge of exasperation or fear. "I'll have to look at my schedule and let you know when I'm off."

She gives me my total, and after I pay she slips me a piece of paper. "Write down your number and I'll text you once I find out."

"Absolutely." I say with a salute.

After getting my order from the end of the counter, I quickly jot down my phone number. I drop it by the register before Derrick and I leave. Once we get to the car, I realize she didn't offer up her number. I'm guessing that was a calculated play. She's either going to back out, or she's going to text me. I really hope it's the latter. Getting rejected over and over by the same girl is starting to sting.

The rain isn't letting up, but I don't want to go back to the dorm. I glance at Derrick and raise my brows. "Where do we want to go? I'm not ready to go home yet. I'm still giving my fingers time to loosen from the zombie ass kicking."

Derrick asks, "Is there a mall around here? I need to pick up a few things if I'm going to have to entertain myself on the off chance Cami actually texts you."

"Yep," I reply. "It'll take about thirty minutes to get there."

"Sounds good," Derrick starts reaching for the radio to turn up the volume.

I press the power button, "No music right now. I need to figure out where I'm going to take her if she agrees."

"Well, what is there to do around here."

I shrug, keeping my eyes focused on the road, trying to make sure I'm far enough away from all the people hauling ass in the middle of a storm. "Not much. I could take her out to eat, but I think after the wait I need to do something epic."

"So, you're setting the bar high for the first date." he questions. "That means all dates after this will have to be equally awesome."

"She's worth it," I say. "She seems like she needs a little bit of happiness in her life. And if I can be the one that gives it to her, then I'll do everything I can to make it happen."

Right when we are exiting a billboard for a quiet little town catches my eye. I've never actually been there, but I've heard nothing but good things. The town has become quite the tourist destination for day trips. Just like that, I know what I want to do on our first official date. I hope she has a full day off, I think we'll need the entire day to do what I have cooking in my brain. I just have to do a little research when we get back home to make sure it's all going to pan out. I didn't think I'd be anxious to be back in my little room, especially since I've been trying to avoid it all day. But now...Now I have plans that need to be made.

cami

I'M STILL stunned when my shift ends. I figured Travis would have been done with me, even after I apologized. I'm still not sure how I feel about it. It's definitely more than a passing crush if I'm still thinking about him as much as I have been.

I checked my schedule before I left Roasted, and I'm off Thursday. I have the paper with his phone number clutched in my fingers, scared if I loosen my grip the tiniest bit the paper will fly away and I'll never be able to give him my response. Or maybe the rain will soak through it and the numbers will become blurred.

I'm kicking myself in the ass for not driving to work today. In my defense, I never check the weather. It was so dark this morning when I left that I couldn't tell if there were clouds. The one drawback to working the early morning shift is that I am not a morning person. I need all the sleep. At least I had my jacket with me, otherwise I'd be completely soaked right now.

Opening the door of my building, I pull my phone out

of my bag. I was planning on calling Tonya on the walk home, but I didn't want to chance ruining my phone. My shoes are squeaking and water is dripping from the bottom of my pants, making a mess across the floor, as I dial Tonya's number.

"Hello," she answers.

"Hey, Little Mama," I say while waiting on the elevator. I don't feel like taking the stairs today. With my luck, I'd slip and fall down them.

Tonya exclaims, "Hey," like she didn't know who was calling. "Sorry, I just finished changing Layla's diaper. I'll be happy when she's old enough to go potty like a big girl."

I laugh. "I think you have quite a few years before that happens."

"If only they were born potty trained," she sighs into the phone. "So, how did your first day of work go?"

"The first day was a little rocky," I admit. "But today, they moved me from restocking to taking coffee orders."

Now, it's Tonya's turn to laugh. "You'll be running that place before you know it."

The elevator dings with its arrival. I swear this is the most run down dorm on campus. Why did my father pick this one for me? Was it to teach me some sort of lesson? If it was, that lesson backfired. Living in this worn out building has given me a pretty awesome friend.

"Yep," I say. "Time for me to conquer the world."

I'm stepping on to the elevator when Tonya asks, "You'll do great." She pauses... "So, whatever happened to that guy? You never mentioned him again."

Damn it. Just when I thought she wouldn't remember, she just has to bring it up. I forget she stores information like a computer. "Do you want the short or long version?" The elevator doors open on my floor. I step out, and lean against the wall.

"Let's go with the short version," she says. "You can give me the longer one when we see each other."

"Okay," I breathe. "He asked me out after I hung up with you that day. I told him only if my roommate could come so that it wouldn't officially be a date. That went okay, but he kept persisting on a date and I freaked out. I went to a party, got myself into an iffy situation, and he literally carried me out. I slapped him."

"So, that bad huh?" She asks.

"There's more... I went to his dorm room to apologize, and he accepted it. I figured he didn't want anything to do with me. But, he came into the coffee shop today, and asked me out again. I told him I'd check my schedule, got his number, but I haven't called him, yet."

Tonya let's out a breath. "Wow, you really know how to get yourself in some awkward moments. How are you even surviving without me?"

"Not funny, T," I say, exasperated.

"First, I want to know what the situation was that he felt he had to carry you out. Second, are you going to call him?"

"I don't know," I scoot down the wall until I'm sitting on the floor. "I want to, but the fact that I have any sort of emotion towards him terrifies me."

Setting my bag down on the floor next to me, I continue, "And the situation wasn't my proudest moment. I got drunk, and started dancing in front of a group of guys. I feel like a complete moron now, but I just didn't want to feel anything at the time."

Tonya takes a breath, filling up her lungs for the "you need to be careful" speech, but I stop her before she has a chance. "I know it was dumb. I don't need a lecture, I get plenty of those from my father. But, I wanted to tell you how ridiculous I've been acting. It's just so hard to keep my insecurities and busy mind at bay between these emotions and dealing with Dad."

"I know, girl. But you have to know that getting shit-faced isn't the answer, right? That's not going to solve anything."

"I know, and I'm trying to sort it all out," I reply. "I need to go; this hallway floor is cold and most likely disgusting. I'll talk to you later."

"Bye, Cam," Tonya says. But before I hang up I hear her last words, "Know that I've got your back, and you don't have to hurt yourself to feel better."

I don't reply. I just hit the red icon on my phone.

Darcy is walking down the hallway when I start opening the door. The crazy, emotional high I was on just twenty minutes ago is dwindling, but Tonya said exactly what I needed to hear. She's always looking out for me, even when she's so far away.

I don't bother closing the door when I walk in knowing Darcy is coming right behind me. I throw my bag on the chair by the desk and lean against my desk, waiting for her arrival.

"What if I was being followed by a serial killer?"

Darcy asks as soon as she's in the room and closes the door. "Then we'd both be goners."

"That is quite possibly the most random thing I've ever heard you say." I reply. "And, I didn't see anyone behind you. I assumed we were safe from all weirdos."

She sets her purse on the nightstand, and turns around to get a good look at me. "What's wrong? You look like someone just stole your dog."

Shrugging, I push aside the assignments on my desk. "Nothing really. I heard some words that I didn't like, but needed to hear from Tonya. But I'm good."

She steps closer to me, squinting, as if that will help her see me better. "Are you sure?"

I nod. "Actually, something happened at the shop today."

"Who's ass do I need to kick?" Darcy yells, taking on a fighter stance, her fists raised in the air. I don't think she realizes she looks adorable more than she looks fierce.

"Calm down, Scrappy," I laugh. "Nothing bad happened... Travis came in, and he asked me on a date."

She's jumping up and down, like she's the one that was asked out. "Please, for the love of all that is Holy, tell me you said yes."

"Not exactly," I say. I keep talking so she doesn't interrupt me. "I had him give me his number so I could text him after I looked at the schedule."

"Well," she asks, bouncing on her toes. "Did you check? Did you call him?"

"I checked the schedule. I'm off Thursday, but I

haven't called him yet." I'm twirling my hair around my finger. "I just don't know how I feel about him."

"What do you mean?"

I release a breath, "I mean, I've never really been the type to actually date anyone. I would casually see people, and when I was bored with them, I'd end it."

I hold up my hand in defense of whatever she's about to say. "I know that sounds horrible, but they knew the stakes. I don't know what to do with these feelings I have for him. They jump from annoyed to interested. Maybe it's because he always seems to be around when I need him."

Darcy is nodding her head, looking like a bobble head doll. "I can understand that. But, he seems like a pretty decent guy. At least, from the one time I've been around him."

I can only agree. He hasn't done anything that would make me worry that he's anything other than a gentleman.

"What do you have to lose if you go on one date with him? Who knows... You may even agree to a second date, or a third." She touches my arm, "Don't close yourself off to new possibilities just because you had a poor role model."

"You are absolutely right," I say. "I'm not going to let my issues with my father affect what I do anymore. That's the whole reason I got a job."

Darcy walks over to my desk, and grabs my phone from I where I set it down. She shoves in my hands, "Call him."

"Okay, okay," I mutter. "You don't have to be so

pushy. I'll text him, though. I might back out if I have to actually say the words."

She's standing over my shoulder, watching me. It's unsettling, but I know she's not going to budge until she knows that I texted Travis.

I add his name to my contacts, and begin typing.

Me: *Hi, this is Cami. The answer to your question earlier is yes. I'm off on Thursday.*

I wait a few seconds that feel like hours, terrified he's not going to respond. Then my phone vibrates in my hand, scaring the hell out of me.

Travis: *Great! I'll pick you up around 9 in the morning. Wear comfortable shoes.*

Wear comfortable shoes? I wonder what he has planned.

Darcy pats my back, "See, was that so hard?"

"Shut it, lady," I reply. "Let's go grab some dinner."

She tosses my bag at me, grabs her purse and opens the door. Before we walk out, she hugs me. "Here's to new possibilities and choosing your own path."

I really need her and Tonya to meet. I can already tell she'll fit right in with us.

travis

EVERYTHING IS LOADED in the back of my car. I put together a picnic lunch for us. It's nothing fancy since I can't afford much, but I hope it will make her happy just the same. At the last minute, I decide to throw in a blanket. I'm not sure what is available at one of the places we're going, so I need to plan ahead.

Derrick is holed up playing video games, as usual. He said he isn't going to stay in the room all day, but honestly, I don't know how much I believe him. He hasn't been all that willing to leave. I'm just happy it stopped raining. I would be in a world of trouble for my date with Cami if it was still pouring the way it has been the last two days. I'm still nervous about how well the area we're visiting today is after all the rain. I hope Cami is wearing comfortable shoes like I asked her to.

It's a couple of minutes before nine when I get to Cami's building. Thank God our buildings are pretty close since I was running late. I didn't think to ask her if she would be waiting for me in the recreation area, or in her room. I'm pulling my phone out of my pocket to text her, but the door to the building opens, and she walks out.

I can't begin to describe how beautiful she is. Her long, brown hair lying in loose curls over her shoulders. She isn't wearing a lot of makeup, only a touch of gloss on her lips. It highlights her mouth, and immediately draws my attention to that area. I want to know how her lips will feel against mine. Will they be as soft as they look? Will she give herself over to me?

When I pull my gaze away from her face, I notice that she definitely took my comfortable shoe advice. She even upped it a notch by wearing capris that look as if they've been painted on her legs, they are so tight. Over her pale pink tank top is a flannel, with the sleeves rolled up to her elbows. I don't think she realizes she's still intimidating, even when she's dressed down.

Cami looks past me, to my car. She has a look of confusion, nose scrunched up and forehead creased. She opens her mouth, but no words come out. A hand goes up to her hair, and fiddles with the ends.

"What?" I ask, trying to hide the hurt. "You didn't think I would have a vehicle."

"It-it's not that," she says. "I just expected it to be a fixer upper."

"Well, it's the first thing I ever bought myself. I made sure to get something that was going to last me a while." I reply, barely keeping the bite out of my voice. It sucks that she thinks so little of me. But, can I blame her? She doesn't really know anything about me.

I open the car door, waiting for Cami to make her

way down the sidewalk. When she is about to slide into the car, I stop her by claiming her hand. "Thank you for agreeing to go on this date with me. I was just about to give up."

She grins, "I guess that means I should have held out a little longer." She winks before getting into my SUV. I close the door gently after her, trying to keep my wide smile to myself. I don't want to scare her off before we've even left the campus.

Not even five minutes into the drive and she's trying to control my radio. She keeps scanning through the channels, listening for anything she might like. Every time she stops, there's heavy drum beats, screaming guitars and singers. Honestly, it's giving me a headache. I don't typically listen to heavy rock. It's just not my thing.

We make a stop in south Austin to get a couple of snacks. I could just go around the back and pull some from the small cooler, but I want to keep that a surprise. We walk into the convenience store and she's looking around like she's not sure what she wants to snack on. I grab a chocolate bar and a big bottle of water. Cami is walking up and down each aisle, inspecting every item. I think she's just trying to take her time.

"You need some help?" I ask.

"Nope," she replies, picking up a bag of gummy bears. "I have what I want."

"Grab you a drink, I'll be at the register when you're ready to get out of here."

I'm barely putting my items on the counter when Cami comes up, puts her arm around mine, and tosses her things on the counter. The small gesture makes my heart race. I feel like I'm dreaming. This girl, that I've liked for a very long time, is here...with me. I'm tempted to pinch myself, but don't in case I wake up from this dream. I'm a little out of my element here.

Before we get back on the road, I hook up my phone to the radio. I like the girl, but I cannot handle what she calls music. I search through my playlists and settle on *Breaking Benjamin*. I feel like it's a good mix between both of our tastes.

As soon as she hears the opening notes of *Failure*, she looks at me in surprise. "You listen to these guys?"

"Yep." I say. "I've even seen them live a couple of times."

She shrieks, "No way."

"They put on a pretty good show." I take a second to look over at her. "Maybe I could take you if they play in Austin again."

"I would freaking love that." Only a few minutes pass before she starts talking again. "Where are you taking me anyway? It's not some secret place where you can hide my body is it?"

"You are beyond morbid." I adjust my seat, leaning it back just a bit. "No, it's not a place I can dispose of your body. But I'm not going to tell you." I whisper, "It's a surprise."

"Pleeeease, tell me," Cami whines. "I'll be your friend forever and ever."

"Nice try, Cami. But, that's not going to work."

"Damn," she mutters. "It was worth a shot."

She sits back and stares out the window, looking at the scenery as we pass it. There isn't much out here. I was hoping there would be something other than hills and trees to keep her from pestering about where we're going.

She's opening her mouth, no doubt prepared to pepper me with questions, when she gasps. "Oh my gosh. We're going to Wimberley. I've been wanting to visit for a while. They have so many cute shops."

"How did you figure out that's where we're going?" I ask.

"The signs, duh. You just have to pay attention to your surroundings." Cami winks at me, then continues to look out the passenger side window.

At least she doesn't know where *exactly* we're going. She may have figured out the town, but this quaint little place has a lot of things to do. I just have to get to the other side of town without her figuring the rest out. If she sees more signs, she's likely to know.

I hand her my phone. "Why don't you control the music the rest of the way? But, maybe something a little less scream-y."

"I can do that," she says. A few seconds later Ed Sheeran's voice comes through the speakers. I glance at her shocked. I wouldn't have pegged her as a pop fan. But I guess there are many layers to this girl that's hardened her heart.

Finally, we get to the pull off for Jacob's Well. The website says it's too cold to swim, but we can still hike the trail. I just hope it's not too muddy to get down there. I've always wanted to see this place, but I'm glad I saved it for something special.

While we're paying to get into the park, the guy in

the booth asks if we'd like a map. "Do we really need one?" I ask.

He looks at me like I'm an idiot. "Have you ever been here before?" I shake my head. "Then I suggest you take one, just in case."

The parking lot is practically empty, except for a few cars parked along the back row. I pick a location pretty close to the park exit. I'm looking at the map trying to figure out where we need to go when Cami snatches it out of my hand.

"Do you really think we need it?" She asks. "It's not like this place is that big."

Opening up the map, she looks over it, turning it in circles a few times. She tilts her head to the side, as if that will give her better insight. It might, but I don't think it's going to work. She pinches her lips together and hands the map back to me. "I think maybe we should take it anyway, in case we get lost."

"Good idea." I reply. I definitely don't want to get lost on any kind of trail. Even though we can't get in the water of the well, I can't wait to see it. I find it fascinating that nobody really knows how far the well goes with all the caves and turns. People have died while diving to explore the area.

I jump out of the car so that I can open Cami's door for her. I know a lot of guys don't do that anymore, but I want to show her that she's special. She should expect nothing but the best out of people. I have a feeling she hasn't received that treatment from many in her life.

Her breath hitches when I pull the door open. She stares at me, slightly dazed. "Are you okay?"

"Yes, it's just...I've never had someone do that for me." she grabs my hand so that I can help her out, gently squeezing it.

Once she's out, we look at the map, heads huddled over it. I glance up to take in our surroundings. There's the booth where we paid our entrance fee. I put my finger on it on the map, make sure it's facing the correct direction. That means the trail to get to Jacob's Well is to the right of that. I fold the map and put it in my back pocket.

"This way." I point to my right.

Crossing the small street, we take in all that nature has to offer us. Cami is excited. I can tell by the way she's bouncing on her toes and grabbing my arm, urging me to walk faster. I'm not sure how the terrain is so I don't want to tire out too fast. I know that can happen on any sort of hiking trail.

The land starts to decline, and I think we're getting close. But we're not. According to the signs and the map, we still have a way to go. There are trees covering so much of the area. The shade is making the air cooler, and I'm glad Cami thought to wear long sleeves.

The trail will even out, then go down again. I'm beginning to wonder if we'll ever get to the well. We come to a set of stairs made of rock. I start walking down with Cami close behind. The closer I get to the bottom, the more slippery the rocks get. Luckily, there's a rail to hold on to or Cami and I would both be tumbling.

This area is extremely shaded, and the path narrows. We can no longer walk side by side. Cami is close behind, hand grabbing ahold of the back of my shirt. The path is even rockier here than it was before and there's a wall of solid rock to the left of us.

When we get past the copse of trees bordering the steep drop off on our right, Cami gasps. When I look down, I can see why. On the side of the cliff, with the creek just on the other side of it, is a hole. The water on the surface is a deep blue, but you can see the water darken just below that. I wonder what it would feel like to jump into that gaping hole, not knowing how far down you go. It must be freeing, letting go of all the worry.

I scoot over a little and grab Cami's hand. "Do you want to go all the way down?"

She shakes her head. "I'm good. That looks a lot steeper than the trails we just walked." She tilts her head to the side. "It's beautiful, though, isn't it?"

I want to tell her that it's not as beautiful as the person standing beside me, but I know that will come off as cheesy, so I just nod in response. This, this is what peace feels like. There's no addict mothers, no party dramas. Just us and nature, giving us a chance to breathe.

cami

A PART of me wants to throw my inhibitions to the wind and jump into the well, even if it's cold. I want to feel that freedom and recklessness. Maybe it will take all the pain and frustration away, and cleanse my soul.

I don't realize just how close I've stepped toward the cliff's edge until I hear Travis call my name. He's looking at the sky, brows wrinkled. I lean my head back and scan the clouds. It looks darker than it was just a moment ago. As if the skies are about to open up and ruin our perfect moment.

Travis turns toward me, with his hand outstretched. "You ready to get out of here?"

I grab his hand and nod. When we're walking through the tiny path to the stairs, something on the rock wall catches my attention. I pull up short to get a better look. There are messages carved into the rock, everywhere. Some are only initials and dates, while others are declarations of love. I feel like I'm getting small glimpses into the lives of these strangers.

"Hey, Travis," I question. "Any chance you have a knife, or something sharp?"

He lets go of my hand and starts patting his pockets. Seconds later he retrieves a pocket knife and places it in my hand. "Try to hurry. I have one more place I want to take you."

"Okay," I reply, and get to work.

I don't want to take too much time. Travis keeps nervously looking toward the horizon. No doubt hoping any bad weather holds off until he can show me the next part of our date.

Finally, minutes later, I'm done. I step to the side, admiring my quick masterpiece. Well, it's not a work of art, just a small reminder that I was here. That this place spoke to me.

Travis looks at the letters I've added to the wall. A small "C & T, 2017" is scratched into the surface. It's not very deep, so I'm not sure how long it will actually be visible. I grab my phone, run back to the cliff edge to snap a shot of the well, and back to the wall taking a picture of my handiwork.

The grin that takes over Travis's face gives me butter-flies. Maybe Darcy was right. What would it hurt to see where things go with him? I'm obviously attracted to him. He also hasn't run off screaming, even though I haven't been all that great to him.

"Are you ready now?" he asks, grabbing my hand once more. It feels comfortable, like my hand was meant for his.

"Absolutely," I say. "Let's go to this other mysterious location you have lined up."

The trek down to Jacob's Well was nothing compared to the inclines we face going back to the car. Good gravy, I did not think I was quite this out of shape. But it was worth it, to see this natural well, to feel the overwhelming peace.

We've just come up the last hill, and I can see the car in the distance. I feel this need to get rid of the pent-up energy I have just being around Travis. I look over at him. He's breathing just as hard as I am. "Race you to the car!" I exclaim.

I don't give him time to respond. Squeezing his hand once, I let go, and take off. I have to do whatever I can to gain the advantage. It's a few seconds before I hear his feet hit the ground behind me. I push harder. I can't lose.

I'm a couple of feet from the car when I feel arms come around me. Travis lifts me off the ground and spins me around before placing me back on the ground next to the car. I turn around and peer into his eyes. I see nothing but hope and kindness in them. How can this guy, who barcly knows me, affect me so much?

The way he's looking at me is intense. He glances to my lips, then back to my eyes. I don't know what he sees there, but I hope it's not the fear I feel rising from my gut. I hope he can't sense how insecure I am, not just about him, but about relationships in general.

He leans his head down, coming closer and closer. I can feel his breath mingling with my own. Right before he lips touch my own, I duck away. I have so many emotions swirling through me. I don't want the confusion to mar this moment. When we kiss, I want it to be perfect.

I see the hurt cross his face. But I can't help it. "We should probably go."

"Yeah," he mumbles, before unlocking the door. I just hope I didn't push him too far away.

* * *

Not even ten minutes later we're pulling into another parking lot. This one has more cars than the one at Jacob's Well. I catch the name on a wooden plaque, "Blue Hole." I've actually heard of this place, and if what's been said is true, there's no way any part of my body is touching that water. It's supposed to be just as cold as Jacob's Well, or colder. No, thank you.

Travis comes around to my side of the car to open the door for me, again. Each time my heartbeat has picked up speed. I've never seen anyone actually do this for someone else. Well, Reaf does it for Tonya, but he doesn't count since I still think he's too good to be true sometimes. In all the years of my parents' marriage, I've never seen my father open a car, or any, door for my mother. It's no wonder I don't know how to react. It's not a norm in my house.

When he grabs my hand, I know that I haven't pushed his patience with my mood shifts. I just wish there was a way to explain that it's not him, it *really* is me. I don't know how to do this. I've never had a steady relationship with anyone, and this is completely new territory for me.

I try to pay for admission into the park since he paid

for the last one, but he bats my hand away. "Cami, if you try to pay again, I will throw your wallet into the creek."

I stare at him. He wouldn't actually do that, would he? But the determination in his eyes suggests that he might. Everything I need is in my wallet, and I'm not going to be jumping into a creek to retrieve it. I quickly slide it into my bag, just in case. I don't want to push my luck.

The walk down to the creek is nice. I love how they have everything set up. On the ramp down, I look to my left. There's a smaller inlet from the creek. It looks like an area for small children to play so they don't get overrun by bigger ones.

There's a large expanse of green grass, surrounded by a sidewalk. There are families playing football, Frisbee, and children running around playing tag. I'm even shocked to see people actually in the creek. It's still pretty chilly here, even if it is March. There's no way you would find me submerged in any kind of water, much less jumping off a rope into the clear water below.

Travis leads me to the edge of the water. There's a rocky outcropping, where we can sit down without getting soaking wet. I set my bag on the ground and sit down with my legs folded beneath me. Travis slides his shoes off, then his socks, stuffing them inside his shoes. He rolls his pants up to his calves.

"What are you doing," I ask.

"What does it look like," he answers. "I'm putting my feet in the water."

"But, why?"

"It's what some people do when they are near water." he deadpans.

He slides his feet into the water. "Come on, Cami. Live a little. It's not like we're going all the way in."

I don't know. I don't really care for water, even in the summer. I'm not a strong swimmer, and I'd rather not drown. But I look at him. Staring at his feet dangling in the water, and moving up his body to his face. He doesn't grimace, or flinch, at the temperature of the water. Maybe it's not that bad.

I slide my legs out from under me and take off my shoes and socks. I don't have to worry about rolling my jeans up since I'm wearing capris. I glance at Travis, one more time, just to make sure he's not actually cold. Scooting forward just a bit, I lower my legs, and plunge my feet into the water.

Immediately, I jump up. How the actual hell is he not freezing? It feels like it's negative twenty. There's no way I'm leaving my feet in that frigid water. That's a sure way to catch pneumonia, or something. I'm bouncing up and down, like that's actually going to warm me up. Travis is busy laughing at my charades. I don't think it's very funny. He could have at least warned me.

"It's so not funny," I bite out.

He holds up his fingers, a tiny space between them, "Just a little bit." He's laughing again, literally slapping his knee. "You should have seen your face."

"You think it's funny...until I push you in." I smirk.

"You wouldn't?"

"I might," I shrug. "I might not. You'll just have to wait and see."

That sobers him up quick. "Come sit down," he pats the space next to him. "You don't have to put your feet in. I'll even take mine out so you don't feel like you need to."

"Your toes can freeze, for all I care." I sit next to him. He pulls his feet out of the water anyway. I think it's actually too cold for him, too. He just wants me to think he's this super macho guy. Nice play, buddy.

"I know it's none of my business," Travis starts, "But why didn't you go home for Spring Break? You must have friends and family you want to see."

Am I really ready to have this conversation. A part of me wants to shut down, but the other part, the bigger one, wants to confide in him. Then he'll know why I react the way I do.

"It's a long story," I run my fingers through my hair. "There are friends I want to see. Family...not so much."

"You don't have family, or you just don't want to be around them?" Travis leans back and stares at the water.

It's as if he knows it's easier to talk if I don't have to look at him. "I don't want to be around them." I sigh, "My father is an absolute control freak, and not in a good way. He tells me what I can and can't do, what I need to major in, and he doesn't want me to argue with him over any of it. It's like my happiness doesn't matter to him. He only sees another asset to add to his accounting firm."

Travis asks, "Has he always been like that?"

"Not really," I shake my head. "When I was younger, he was a man I looked up to. I didn't pay attention to how he controls every aspect of our lives. It got worse when I started high school. He started putting these demands on me when it came to my grades and extra-curricular activities.

"When it came time to apply for college, he gave me a small stack of approved universities. None of them out of state, so that he could keep me on his leash. The day you found me at that party? I had just gotten a text from my mother saying I was expected to come home and intern at his accounting firm. He didn't even have the balls to call me himself."

Travis is silent beside me, giving me the time I need to work through my thoughts. I stare at the water, wondering what it would feel like to be constant flowing. There's almost nothing that can stop it aside from a freeze and drought.

"That is why I found a job. Why I'm trying to separate myself from them as much as I can. I don't want to live under his thumb. I don't want to live my life according to his rules.

"It's also why I've put off going on a date with you. I didn't want to put myself in a position to be controlled by yet another person."

Travis places his hand under my chin, lifting it until my eyes meet his. "I would never tell you what you can or can't do. I'm good with you being your own person. Life would be boring if you weren't *you*."

I take his hand in both of mine. "That means more to me than you could possibly know. Thank you for letting me get it all out. Even Tonya only knows a part of it."

Just as I'm scooting closer to him, I feel sprinkles hit my face. I look up, letting the light drops take away my frustrations. The sky opens up and we are being drenched by the rain. Travis stands up, gripping my hand. I grab my bag as he's picking up his shoes. He doesn't bother putting them on. We sprint toward the car. I've never felt as free as I do in this moment.

travis

THE RAIN IS PELTING US. It's cold and completely soaking us, but it's exhilarating. Even with the sudden downpour, I've never had this much fun on a date. I've never felt this connected to someone. I may have been worried that she was like my mom, but she has issues just like the rest of us. I do wish she would channel her frustrations better, but I'm not going to tell her what to do. I can't. Especially after hearing the pain and resentment in her voice when she talked about her dad.

I rush to the passenger side of the car to unlock the door, and usher Cami in before I get in on the driver's side. I can see Cami shivering, even though she's laughing just as hard as I am. I don't think she's had this much fun in a while. At least, not while she's sober. It's adorable how much joy she's finding in the little things. But that's what I hope she realizes, happiness in the little things will make everything else feel that much better.

I'm turning the dial on the heater, trying to get the

car warm as quickly as possible. "I'm sorry our date was cut short. I didn't think to check the weather before I planned it." I shrug, "I was hoping we were done with rain after the other day."

Cami is working hard to get her laughter under control, "It's okay. It's not like the meteorologist is ever actually right."

The car goes silent. It feels heavy and intense, like we're waiting on something to happen. The only thing I can hear is the heat blowing through the vents on the dash. I reach for the knob on the radio, something to break up the awkwardness. It reminds me of those moments when you're speaking in front of a crowd, and you don't know what to do with your hands. They just kind of hang there by your side. That's me, right now, trying to figure out how to go forward after the heavy discussion we just had.

I look at Cami, amazed that even soaking wet she's just as beautiful, inside and out. She doesn't realize everything she brings to the world. She doesn't know just how special she is.

I'm about to ask her if she wants to head back to Hilltown, but the words die on my lips. Cami leans toward me and kisses me. It's just a peck at first, but starts to turn into something more. Her hands gravitate toward the back of my neck, playing with my hair. Her lips move over mine, soft, sweet, hesitant.

I'm taken by surprise, especially after the way she dodged me earlier. I was also a little hurt. I thought I was reading the signals she was giving me, but was shot down. Now...I'm glad I didn't push her. She needs to go at her own pace. This, right now, is amazing and perfect.

I wrap my arms around her waist, trying to pull her as close to me as possible with the console between us. I feel her smile against my lips, and can't help my own in return. It makes kissing hard for a second as our teeth clash together. I feel like I'm back in junior high, figuring out how to go about my first kiss. Soon, our lips are sealed together. I can feel her breaths quicken. My tongue teases her mouth open, just slightly. She tastes like mint and gummy bears. This may become my new favorite flavor. She jumps in surprise, but she keeps kissing me right back. Slowly, I reign myself in. I brush my lips against hers once, twice, before pulling back.

"I'm sorry," I say. "I didn't mean to maul you there at the end."

She laughs, a deep belly laugh. "It's all good. I practically attacked you."

"You can attack me any time," I grin.

"I bet you say that to all the girls," Cami bats her eyelashes. She looks like a debutante with all the effort she's putting into the action.

"Number one, stop doing that freaky thing with your lashes. It's weird," I brush a piece of hair behind her ear. "Number two, not really. I don't even remember the last time I've dated anyone. I've had my eyes set on a certain someone for quite some time."

Pink tinges her cheeks. She knows it's her, and I love that I affect her the same way she does me. My dreams of her being here, by my side, have actually come true. I just hope I can keep her fears at bay long enough for her to trust me completely.

A few beats of silence pass, "I, uh, packed a picnic lunch for us. I was planning on eating on the lawn inside Blue Hole, but the rain pretty much killed that idea."

"Really," she's bouncing in her seat. "What did you bring? I'm starving."

I love how she can go from kissing me, like I'm the oxygen she needs, to complaining about being hungry. "Calm down, it's nothing fancy. I'm not sure where we're going to eat it, though."

Cami glances around the car, realizing that the cooler must be in the cargo area. "Do your seats fold down?"

"Yeah, I think so," I reply. "I've never put them down, so I'm not sure how."

She's on her phone typing furiously. I have no idea why she pulled it out so quickly. Maybe she's telling one of her friends how weird I am for not knowing how to work my own vehicle. A few seconds later she shoves her phone in my face. There's a video showing me exactly what I need to do. The people are outside the vehicle putting the seats down, but I bet I can do it within the car. I'm just now drying off, and I don't really want to get pelted with rain anymore today.

A few minutes and a couple of bumps later, I have the seats folded down, the blanket spread out, and our food unpacked. She's sitting with her legs crossed against the hatch, and I'm leaning awkwardly between the front seats. I want to make sure she has all the room she needs to stretch out.

After taking a bite of her sandwich, she moans. Who

knew eating could sound so sexy. There's mayo on the corner of her mouth, and I lean over to wipe it off.

"Thank you," she mumbles around the food in her mouth. After swallowing she says again, "Thank you. I'm not usually such a messy eater."

"It's okay. It's kind of cute," I reply.

"I think this just proves I'll never survive a zombie apocalypse. I don't think I'd do well with going hungry. You'd probably hear my stomach growling over the zombies moaning and shuffling."

I laugh. I can't think of any way to follow up that response. Her sense of humor is dark, but also funny in a way I wasn't expecting.

Once we finish eating, we throw all the trash into the cooler. I try folding the blanket in the small confines of my car before giving up and throwing it in a pile. I don't even bother putting the seats back up before we climb back into the front. The rain has slowed down, and I want to get on the road before the traffic through Austin is horrible. It's almost always bad, but bad weather makes it ten times worse.

On the drive home Cami grabs my phone and finds a comedy station. She grabs my hand and winds her fingers through mine, before placing our joined hands in her lap. Our trip back is more intimate, and I can't help but feel like our stars have finally aligned.

cami

TRAVIS PULLS UP to my building. I'm not ready to let the night end. I've had a lot of fun today, more fun than I've had since I was back home with Tonya. He lets go of my hand briefly so that he can put the car into park, then grabs it once more. I have a feeling he doesn't want the night to end either.

I pout, looking through my lashes. "Does this date really have to end?"

Chuckling, Travis says, "We can go somewhere else if you want, but, I should probably go check on Derrick."

I raise my eyebrow in question. Why would he have to check on another grown person?

"He's like a puppy," he shrugs. "If you leave him alone for too long, he can cause destruction."

"Did you just compare your friend to a dog?" I snort.

"A dog might have better manners than he does," he replies.

I'm still not ready to go, but I guess I'll let him get back to his friend. They only have the rest of the week to spend together. I know if it was Tonya that was here, I probably wouldn't have agreed to the date in the first place. I know how important it is to be around those you care about as much as you can.

I feel a sharp pang in my stomach. I miss Tonya. She's the one I would be rushing to tell about my date. I still can, but it's not the same when I can't see her in person.

Reluctantly, I reach for the door handle. Travis rips his hand from mine, jumps out of the driver's seat, and rushes to my door. It's amazing how much effort he puts into proving that he's a gentleman.

He's breathing heavy, chest rising and falling rapidly. "Are you ready to be done with me?" he pants.

I shrug, "I don't know. I don't want to make things weird."

"Well," he laughs, "You definitely did that by reaching for the door without saying anything."

He pulls me to him and wraps his arms around me. I burrow my face into his chest. His shirt is still damp from the earlier rain. I breathe in his scent. Right now, he smells like outside and sweat, but I can catch whiffs of the light cologne he usually wears. And the fact that I know what he usually smells like scares the hell out of me.

He leans back. "Did you just sniff me?"

I hide my face in his shirt, hoping he doesn't see my embarrassment. There's no doubt the tips of my ears are a bright shade of scarlet. But, of course, he does. He lifts my head and gently places his lips against mine.

The kiss is soft and quick. I want to pull him back to me, and kiss him with the ferocity I feel inside. I've never had another person bring out this kind of emotion, or passion, in me. Not like he does, anyway.

He's staring into my eyes. "Don't ever feel bad for anything you do or feel." He pauses for a beat, making sure I'm paying attention. "Besides, it was kind of adorable."

I poke him in the side, wanting to get some kind of reaction from him since he pretty much just made fun of me. But he did it in a way that I know he's laughing with me, not at me. There's a difference, after all. He winks at me before kissing my forehead, and pulling back.

I already feel cold and insecure without his arms holding me to him. Am I turning into a stage five clinger? No way. I'm the one that keeps guys at a distance. I don't cling to someone, especially someone I'm just getting to know. But, I can't hide my feelings toward him. Even if they are conflicted.

He turns to his car, "I'll text you later."

"Okay," I say, meekly. I can't find my voice. Travis makes me speechless, which has never happened before. I place my fingers over my mouth. I can still feel the weight of his lips over mine, and how perfect it felt.

I barely have the door to my room open when my phone dings.

Travis: *Sooooo, I was thinking… Would you and Darcy like to join Derrick and me on a double date Saturday?*

Cami: *I'll have to ask her when she gets home. I'm not sure when that'll be.*

I stand there for a second, door wide open, to think. There's no way he's already made it back to his building. I walk to the window and pull back the curtain. There he is, looking up and through his windshield, directly at my window.

> **Cami:** *Creeper, much?*
> **Travis:** *I wanted to make sure you made it to your room okay.*
> **Cami:** *You could have walked me up…*
> **Travis:** *True, but then I wouldn't have left.*
> **Cami:** *Is that such a bad thing?*
> **Travis:** *Not at all.*

This is ridiculous. We are having a conversation through messages while staring at each other. I wave, and point my finger down to let him know I'm coming back downstairs. This feels like a modern-day *Romeo & Juliet*, without the death, and only a little bit of angst. He holds his hand up to stop my movements. Seconds later my phone vibrates in my hand.

> **Travis:** *Don't come down. I'm going for real, now.*
> **Cami:** *Are you sure?*
> **Travis:** *Yep, puppy-like person, remember?*
> **Cami:** *Okay. I'll talk to you later then?*
> **Travis:** *Absolutely. Don't forget to let me know what Darcy says.*

I send him a "thumbs up" emoji, and put my phone on my desk. It dings again, and I can't help the grin that takes over my face. There's nothing that can bring me down right now. Only, that changes as soon as I see who sent the message.

Dad: *I expect you home this weekend.*

My stomach drops. How is it that the person who helped create me can make me feel so small and insignificant? Isn't he supposed to build me up and support me? I've always been jealous of Tonya's relationship with her parents. She has the family situation I always dreamed I would have. It's why I spent so much time at her house. Her parents welcomed me, and treated me like I was their own. Tonya always joked that I was the sister she never had. Instead, I'm stuck with a controlling asshole for a father. It's his way, or no way. The *great* Benjamin Alexander should take notes from the Burgess family.

My mom isn't much better. She's let him control every aspect of our lives. She knows how I feel. She knows I don't want to go into accounting. I'm not sure what I want to do, but I'd like the chance to explore my options. It would just be nice if she stood up for me every once and a while. If she tried to get my father to see my side of things. But when he says "jump," she asks, "how high."

I can feel the tension, and stress, building in my neck and along my shoulders. My hand reaching for the pills I've relied on for so long to get through the feelings my parents bring up. But I stop myself, just now realizing I haven't taken my medicine in a few days. I've managed just fine without them. I'm not going to let *them* be the reason I fall back into my old patterns.

Instead of focusing my energy on my father's demands, I decide to look at the pictures I took on my adventure with Travis today. I lie down on my bed, with my legs resting up and against the wall, my head toward the foot of the mattress. My legs are sore from the hike at Jacob's Well, and running through the rain at Blue Hole, having them against the wall feels great. I can feel my muscles stretching, relieving some of the ache.

I swipe through my photos, smiling as I look at each one. I come to the picture of my rock carving, and decide to save it as my wallpaper. Not so much because of the "C & T" part, but because I felt something when I was there. I felt free, and I want to remember that even when unwanted texts pop up. It's a reminder to breathe, and not let the things I can't control bring me down.

I don't have anything else to do, and I'm bored. I'm not used to this much alone time. Even before Darcy and I became close, she was always here in some aspect. I grab my *Buffy* DVD's, select the disc for season one, and put it into the player. Leaning back on my pillow, I smile when the opening song starts to play. It feels weird watching it without Tonya. It doesn't matter anyway, I'm so comfortable that I drift off to sleep.

* * *

There's a loud slam, and I jump out of bed, worried someone, or something, is about to attack me. Yes, I said *something*. Tonya's great-grandmother tells some scary ass stories about monsters coming to get you if you don't go to bed. I miss that fiery woman. Tonya and I need to take a road trip to see her soon, maybe we can bring Darcy along for the ride.

Darcy is storming through the room, thank goodness. If it had been something wishing to do me harm, I'd be screwed. Maybe next time I shouldn't let my thoughts drift away. She throws her purse on the bed. It bounces before falling over the side, and spilling everything onto the floor. She's slamming doors for no reason at all. I haven't seen her take anything out, or put anything in them.

If I'm being honest, she's acting like I usually do. And, if I look that fucking ridiculous in the process, I want to kick her ass for not making me calm my ass down. It's funny, and it takes everything in me to stop the laugh from escaping my lips. Apparently, I don't do a very good job because a giggle slips through. Darcy whips around and glares at me.

"What," I ask. "It's funny. You don't normally act like me. I don't see how you aren't always laughing when I come crashing through the room."

She rolls her eyes, not even responding, and goes back to slamming stuff around. "Seriously, though. Who pissed in your cereal?"

"Ugh," she grunts. "People of the male species are assholes."

"I'm guessing it was a bad day at work." I get comfortable on my bed now that I know I'm not going to die a horrible, excruciating death. Well, I won't rule it out because if looks could kill, the one I'm receiving from Darcy right now would put me six feet under.

"That is an understatement. This jerk came in and spent the whole day in the shop." She slams the closet door this time. "That's not a bad thing, though. He kept coming up to the counter when I had a line of people to ask for stupid shit that can be found on the condiments table."

Darcy takes a deep breath, trying to center herself. I'm covering my mouth trying to hide my smile, and the laugh waiting to burst out. "If he had only done it once, it would be forgivable, but he came up there every freaking time I was busy. He *refused* to let anyone else help him."

This time I do laugh. "Maybe he likes you."

She throws a scarf at my head. "This isn't the fucking third grade. You don't constantly annoy a person to get their attention. You wait until there's a lull in the crowd, and then come talk to them like a civilized fucking adult."

Wow, I don't think I've ever heard her curse as much as she has in the past five minutes. It makes me feel a tiny bit better to know that I'm not the only one that loses her chill. It can happen to anyone, even the always happy, always positive Darcy.

"You need to calm down, girlfriend. And, I know just the thing to help." I get up, grab a bag of popcorn from my snack drawer, toss it in the microwave, and punch the auto-timer. While that's cooking, I put the already playing *Buffy* back on the start menu. I listen for the popcorn to be done. It's a science, and the microwave never gets it right. When the pops start slowing down, I remove the bag and dump it in a huge bowl I keep on my desk for these occasions.

I pat my bed, "Park it, sister. We are going to get our *Buffy* on."

She looks at me with confusion. "I don't think I've ever watched this show. Isn't it ridiculously old?"

I gasp, "You've never seen this?" Darcy shakes her head. "Well, get your ass over here. I'm about to pop your *Buffy* cherry."

While the theme song is playing, I place the bowl of popcorn between us. "Tonya is the one that got me hooked on this show. Well, her mom, too. Any time either of us had a bad day, she would put it on and tell us 'Seeing an awesome chick kick some booty will brighten any day.'"

I'm hit with another pang of longing. I miss them both so much, even Mr. Burgess. They are where I will always consider *home*. I still haven't called Tonya to tell her about my date, but I'll wait until tomorrow. Darcy is the one that needs me right now.

About half-way through the second episode Darcy speaks up. "They were right. I feel a little bit better now."

"I told you."

She grabs the remote and hits pause. "In all my fit throwing, I forgot to ask you how everything went today. I'm going to take a wild guess it went well since you haven't found the closest party to escape to."

I cringe. I hate that I've given her this view of me, even if it's true. "It actually went really well. He wants to go out again on Saturday, but with you and his friend as a double date."

Darcy groans and bangs her head against the wall. "I don't think I'm ready to interact with the male species on a personal level any time soon."

"Please," I beg. "Besides you kind of owe me."

A feel a piece of popcorn hit the side of my head. "How do you figure that?"

"Because," I shrug. "I introduced you to the awesome qualities of a teenage vampire slayer."

She laughs, and almost spills the rest of the popcorn on my bed. "I guess," she pauses, "But if it goes south, you owe me."

"Deal." I hold my pinkie up, waiting for her to hook her pinkie around mine, and we make the most sacred of oaths. The pinkie promise.

I don't know what she's so scared of. What could possibly go wrong?

travis

DERRICK IS ACTUALLY EXCITED to get out of the room and go out with Cami and Darcy. He's been acting weird since I came home from my date on Thursday. When I pressed why he was in such a good mood, he didn't say anything. He just kept playing the stupid video game with a smile on his face.

That crazy smile is still on his face, and I don't know if I should be happy about it, or worried. You never really know with him. He's generally a happy guy, but there are times when he goes above and beyond annoying when he gets an idea stuck in his head.

"You ready," I call over my shoulder, trying to get my jacket on. We're going to a Mexican restaurant, and while I know I don't have to dress up, I want to. I need Cami to know she's getting the full package when it comes to dating me.

Derrick grunts in response. When I turn around, he's struggling to get a tie on. Where the hell did he get a tie? I don't even own one. "You know, when I said to dress up a little, I didn't mean you had to go all business suit. A nice pair of jeans and a shirt would have worked just fine."

"Oh, *now* you tell me," he bites out. "I'm going to change." He yanks the tie over his head and tosses it across the room.

He's rifling through his suitcase, no doubt trying to figure out which of his clothes are clean and which are dirty. I told him to wash some of them, but he doesn't know how. And, I'm not going to do it for him. If he's serious about coming here next semester, he's going to have to learn how to do basic things. He's not going to have his mom here to do it for him.

While he's busy I send a text to Cami.

Travis: *We're going to be a few minutes late. Derrick's having a clothing crisis.*

Not even seconds pass before the little bubbles appear, showing she's typing me a message.

Cami: *Crisis as in he can't find anything to wear, or clothing optional?*

I find it funny that she would even jump to the other conclusion. She's only met Derrick once, and it's like she already knows exactly how he can be. I bet he'd actually ponder going without clothes.

Travis: *He can't find anything to wear. Thank God it's not the other.*

Cami: *I'm almost ready. We'll be waiting!*
Travis: *Ok. I'll try to get him to hurry up.*

"Are you ready yet, Derrick?" I ask again. I swear I wait on him more than I have any girl I've dated. He takes forever to get ready. He's taking longer this time, though. I feel like he knows something that I don't, and that worries me.

He walks out of the closet in *my* clothes. When did he go to the closet? I couldn't have been in my own head for that long. But I was because while we were texting, I was remembering that hopeful spark in her eyes when I finally left her dorm parking area. I want to make sure that spark stays there. She should always have something to hope for and look forward to.

"Yep," he claps his hand on my shoulder. "Let's get out of here."

The drive to Cami's takes all of five minutes. Derrick hasn't said a single word. I'm starting to sweat, wondering what he's about to do, or what he has planned.

It feels like Fall, even though we are headed toward the end of March. The night is perfect for a light jacket, though I hope Cami forgets hers so I can be the one to keep her warm. I'm starting to rethink this whole double date thing. Maybe I should have just waited until Derrick was gone so I could have her all to myself. But the guilt that I'd rather spend time with a girl I'm crushing on, possibly even falling for, than with my best friend hits me. Even if he's annoying at times, he's always had my back.

I open the door, and the RA is already shaking her head at me. She's seen me way too many times, and usually when Cami was pissed at me. I don't think I rank very high on her list of people she likes. "Let me go call her down." Before she leaves the room for the office she calls back, "Wait here."

It's a demand, not a request. I contemplate waiting, but ultimately decide I'd rather go straight to Cami's door to pick her up for our date. Last time, she met me outside. This time, it needs to feel like a proper date. Well, except the part where I meet her parents when I pick her up. From what she's told me, I could give a rat's ass what her father says about me dating her.

After a long, excruciating ride in the ancient elevator, we are finally at Cami's door. I knock twice, then stand back and wait. I can hear mumbling coming from the other side. It sounds like they are arguing.

Then I hear Cami say, "You promised not to be all mopey." And, it makes me laugh. It's so close to the words Darcy told her when we went bowling. I'm not sure what put Darcy in a bad mood, so much like the ones I only ever saw on Cami, but I hope she ends up having a good time.

"Fine," Darcy exclaims. Then the door is opening, Darcy is standing in the open doorway with her mouth gaping open and a glare that could melt icebergs. It's not directed at me, but to the person behind me. "YOU," she shrieks and slams the door in our faces.

I look at the closed door, then back at Derrick, wearing a Cheshire smile. "I take it you two know each other?"

He shrugs, "You could say that. I met her the other day when you abandoned me." I roll my eyes and open my mouth to argue with him. "I'm just kidding, I told you to go. But I met her, and she fascinates me."

"Is that why you've been in such a good mood lately?"

He nods in agreement, and knocks on the door, again. We're both standing close to it, trying to hear the hushed conversation happening on the other side. I want to know what's going on, but it's clear they aren't opening the door until they come to some sort of agreement.

I hear someone stomping around the room, then Cami is there with the door open and a smirk on her face. "It's not nice to listen in on conversations."

Derrick tries to enter the room, but Cami puts her hand up, stopping him with that one action. "Just give her a minute." She closes the door, grabs my wrist, and drags me a short distance down the hallway.

"Did you know they knew each other," she whispers.

I shake my head. "He wouldn't tell me why his mood had gone from happy to crazy excitement. At least, now I know why."

"We better get back in there," Cami says. "If we don't, we may walk in to a murder scene. Darcy was not amused with him when she came home Thursday."

Luckily, there's no blood anywhere. When we get into the room, Darcy is on one side and Derrick the other. She's staring him down, and he's gazing at her with amusement. I already have a gut feeling that tonight is either going to be hilarious, or brutal. Too bad it's most likely going to be the latter.

The evening doesn't disappoint. The only thing that would make it better is alcohol, but we're underage, so that's out. Darcy ignored Derrick the entire way to the restaurant. It was only fifteen minutes away, but the silence in the car made it seem like an eternity. It only worsened from there. If Derrick tried to talk to her, she'd either act like he didn't exist or come back with some snippy response.

We're waiting for the check to come so we can get out of here. Cami has her head on the table, trying her best to hide her embarrassment. Derrick is still trying to engage Darcy in conversation. She is still ignoring him, though I think he's starting to wear her down, but not in a good way. I'm worried if she does actually speak, it will be in the form of yelling. And, it may not all be nice words.

Finally, the waiter comes with the bill. I know he can see my sigh of relief. Derrick tries to make a grab for the small folder, but I don't let him take it. This was my bright idea, and I plan on following it through.

When we get to the car, Cami grabs Darcy's hand and leads her in the back seat to sit with her. I'm not happy to have Cami in the back, but it's probably best to keep the other two separated. I look back at Cami, she looks exhausted, and I don't blame her. She's whispering quietly with her best friend.

I glance over at Derrick. "I'm going to take you home, first. Is that okay?"

He just nods, dejected. He comes off a little strong

and he's really loud. I don't think he knows what "inside voice" means. I feel bad for him, really I do, but I'm also a little pissed that it messed up my evening with Cami. I thought it would be fun, clearly I was wrong. I hope she lets me make it up to her after we drop our friends off.

Derrick gets out of the car with a fist bump and a nod. Next is Darcy. I don't want her to be mad at me. If I'd known, I would have told Derrick to hang back, or just rescheduled. She just looks frustrated. Her brows are pinched together, and there's weariness in her eyes. Like going to dinner completely drained her energy. But I understand, even without knowing all the facts.

Instead of pulling up in front of the building to let them out, I park in the lot to the side. Cami looks at me through the rearview mirror, eyebrows raised. I come around and open the back door for both Darcy and Cami. Darcy smiles at me, the first one I've seen all night, "Chivalry isn't dead."

My cheeks flame in embarrassment. "Nope." I wait until they are beside me. "And, I'm sorry for whatever Derrick did to make you mad. He's a lot to handle at the best of times."

Darcy places a hand on my forearm and pats it twice. "No need for you to apologize, you aren't the one that acted like an overgrown idiot." She turns to Cami, "I'm going to the room, I'll see you later." She gives her a big squeezing hug, and walks toward their building.

I grab Cami's hand, "Want to go for a walk?" She shivers. From my touch or the temperature, I don't know, but I grab a jacket from the back of the car and drape it over her shoulders.

"Thanks," she mutters. I should insist on her changing before we walk around the quad, but she looks amazing. With everything going on with Darcy and Derrick, I didn't get to enjoy the view much. She's wearing a dress with skulls on it. The top is tight-fit, showing just a hint of cleavage. The bottom flairs out. It looks like a vintage sundress, and I want her to wear more like them. They show off a sweet, but sassy side of her. A side, I'm sure, not many get to see. She didn't pair the dress with heels, like most would have, instead she has a pair on Converse that match the turquoise skulls. She is unlike any person I have ever met. Even when she feels unsure of herself, she's still her own person.

We start walking out of the parking lot. I'm happy she wore comfortable shoes, it will give us more time together. "Why is Darcy so pissed?" We're strolling along the sidewalk hand in hand, and it feels like we've done this a million times before.

She's so quiet, I don't think she's going to answer. "Darcy is a fun person, but when she's at work, she's insanely serious. Like she doesn't take crap from anyone. From what she says, he was rude and annoying."

That sounds like him. I sigh, there's not really much else I can do. "I can actually picture that. He doesn't mean to be that way, it's just how he's wired. He doesn't know when enough is enough."

"I would suggest he stay away from her, at least, until she calms down." She drifts closer to me, and grabs my arm with her free hand. The feeling I get when she's holding on to me, like I'm her safe place, is amazing. I want to be her safety net in whatever capacity she'll allow.

We round the first corner of the quad. I figured more people would be on campus, even if it is Spring Break. But, the space is empty except for a few stragglers tossing a ball around in the grassy lawn.

"We talked about my family, or mostly my dad, during our last date. What about your family?" Cami asks, glancing my direction before turning back to watch the two guys throw the ball.

She jumps right into it. I don't like talking about my mom, she was a shit parent, and still is. But, she unloaded her feelings when it comes to her dad. It's only fair that I tell her about my strained relationship with my mother.

"It's not a great story," I say.

"It's okay, just give me the short version."

"Well," I start. "I don't know my dad. Hell, I'd be surprised if my mom knows who my dad is. She's not the best mom in the world. She's battled alcohol and drug addiction for as long as I can remember. She still goes on benders. I feel shitty that I can't help her, but I'm at the point where enabling her isn't an option anymore. I can't keep giving her money when I don't have anything to give." I pause, giving her a second to absorb what I've said.

"That's why I'm so close to Derrick, and put up with his obnoxious ass. His family saved me. They gave me a place to stay and food to eat. They took care of me when my own mother wouldn't."

Cami stops, abruptly. She throws her arms around

my neck and pulls me close. "That's why you get so upset when I get sloppy drunk? You're worried I'll end up like her?"

I can only nod. I don't have the words to tell her how much this moment means to me. Or how happy I am that she finally understands why I get so crazy when she's out there drinking without thinking of the consequences.

We're wrapped up in each other when I feel, and hear, her yawn against my neck. I'm still not ready for the night to end, but I don't want to keep her out late. Especially if she has to work tomorrow.

"Let's head back to your dorm."

She starts to argue, but another yawn escapes her lips. "Okay."

We take the stairs to her floor. I don't want to be stuck on that elevator again, and this way is much faster. Cami is practically falling asleep on her feet. She opens the door, leans in and kisses my cheek. "Thank you for a great night."

"Any night, even with drama, is good if I'm with you." I frame her face with my hands, and kiss her. Her arms are wrapped around my waist, and her fingers are digging into my sides. I slide my tongue against her bottom lip, and she opens up. Exploring my mouth as much as I am hers.

A throat clearing behind her has us jumping apart. Darcy is standing there, barely hiding her sly smile. At least she's still okay with this new relationship, even if she hates my friend.

"Goodnight, Travis," Cami gives my hand a gentle squeeze.

"Night," I say before turning around and practically sprinting down the staircase. Tonight may have started out rocky, but that kiss sealed the deal with my heart. I don't know that I'll be able to shake her when she breaks my heart.

cami

IT'S BEEN two weeks since our disastrous double date. Travis and I have spent as much time together as possible. My crush on him grows each time we've gone out. There's still a tiny voice in the back of my mind telling me it won't last. That he'll find me lacking, just like almost everyone else in my life. I quickly shut that voice up. I don't need that kind of negativity in my life. It'll just lead me back down into a deep, dark void.

I just left my morning shift at Roasted. I'm amazed at the fact that I'm starting to balance work, school, and this new relationship so well. It's completely unlike me. I'm a fly by the seat of my pants kind of girl. I've never been one to have a set schedule, except for the ones my father placed on me. My free time was just that, free. I find that I'm starting to enjoy working, and the freedoms it will allow me. The joy it's going to bring when I don't have to answer to anyone but myself.

The walk home is refreshing. Spring is in the air, flowers are blooming and it's starting to warm up. Ask me how my walk is a month from now, and I'm sure I'll be wishing for Winter again. I'll probably drive to work once it goes from warm to "I can't take off enough clothes" hot. I don't have to be anywhere right this second so I take my time. Since my trip to Wimberley with Travis, I've appreciated nature more. I enjoy the calm it brings me, and try to do as much as I can outside.

The room is frigid when I walk in, proof that Darcy has been here at some point this morning. I'll never understand why she has to have it so freaking cold in here. I have to wear a parka just to be comfortable. Ah well, things could be worse. I could have a roommate from Hell. I'll take Darcy any day, even if she's going to turn me into a snowman.

Travis and I have a date later tonight, so I have quite a bit of time to kill. I take a quick shower to get the smell of coffee beans off of me. I love coffee, and working at Roasted, but the smell when I leave…not so much. It clings to my skin, and it seems like it never goes away. I'm my very own caffeine boost. That's not entirely a bad thing with finals and exams coming up in just over a month.

Now that I'm clean, I can work on a few other things. I pull out my assignments for Accounting and get to work on them. Best to get the most hated class out of the way before I move on to something else and lose my motivation.

When I'm tired of looking at "T charts" and ledgers, I close my book, and toss it on the bed. I open my laptop and start looking through the financial aid applications I found over Spring Break. I meant to get them filled out before now, but my time has been consumed by school, work, and Travis. It completely slipped my mind. The deadlines written in red on the white board above my desk remind me that time is running out. Some of the forms are confusing, and they want my parents' financial information. I don't have it, and I'm not calling to ask them for it because I'll be denied if I go that route. I put in my meager wages, and hope they can help me out. I also fill out a couple of scholarship applications, cutting and pasting parts of my entrance essays.

Darcy walks in, setting a massive textbook on her desk, and plops down on her bed. She looks exhausted. There are dark circles under her eyes, and she's paler than normal.

"Is everything okay?" I ask.

"Yeah," she sighs. "This chemistry class is going to kill me if the people in my study group don't do it first."

"That bad, huh?"

"Yep," she sits up and looks around like she doesn't remember the last time she was in here. "What do you have going on tonight?"

"Travis is taking me out," I smile. It's a big, cheesy grin if the groan coming from Darcy is any indication. I can't help it, I really like him. He's so different from other guys I've hooked up with. And that, right there, is the biggest difference in this whole thing. I'm not just hooking up with him. I'm dating him, exclusively. It's a first for me. I've never given anybody that kind of power over my heart.

Darcy gets off her bed and walks to the closet, shuffling her clothes around. "You have fun with that." She takes out a mini skirt, then a sparkly tank top, and throws them on the bed. "I'm going out. I'm not sure what time I'll be back, but don't wait up."

I laugh. It's weird for her to be the one needing the night out. Our roles have reversed, and I wish I could find someone that she could be happy with. If Derrick wasn't the complete opposite of her, I would push for that. I know that would drive her insane so I don't bother bringing it up.

Darcy heads out about an hour later, and I start getting ready. I'm not a hundred percent sure where we're going, but I decide on dressing casual. I've got on light colored skinny jeans, an off the shoulder blue and white, striped shirt, and my Chucks. I figure this is a nice enough outfit for anywhere he plans on taking me.

It's a little after seven, and I text him that I'll be ready in thirty minutes. I begin putting up my make-up so that I can fix my hair right before he gets here. But when I'm done with my make-up, I haven't heard my phone ding. I check it, make sure it isn't on silent before texting him again.

Cami: *I'm just about finished, are you on your way?*

I set my phone down, and play with my hair, trying to figure out how I want to wear it. In the end, I throw it into a messy bun. It's cute, and didn't take a lot of effort. I check my phone again, but there's still no response.

I'm starting to get antsy. He's never not replied before, and is usually pretty quick when I text him. I pick up the phone and call him. I don't call him very often because I don't like talking on the phone. I've never understood why people spend hours on the phone. The only person I ever call is Tonya, but that's because of distance. If she wasn't so far from me, I'd text her like I usually do, or just stop by her house.

The call goes straight to voicemail. I know we are just at the beginning of whatever this is, but he could at least answer. This isn't like him. He has done everything he can to show that he's a gentleman, and that I'm important. What if something happened?

Or, a small voice says, *what if he didn't care for you as much as you thought he did?* I wish I could shut that voice up, that I wasn't insecure. But I've spent years never being good enough for my parents. It's hard to wipe that kind of thinking from my head. Once you've been told you aren't enough, or you need to do better, you start to believe it. I wouldn't blame Travis if he doubted our relationship. What does he want with a head case like me?

I can feel myself spiraling down. I know I should fight the urge to lose myself in alcohol and pills. I haven't had to take my anxiety meds in over three weeks. And that's with my father's passive aggressive messages. But being ignored by Travis is messing with me. I feel rejected. I'll never be what other people want, or need, me to be.

If this was normal, I would brush it aside. But it's not, especially not for him. Doubt swirls through my mind, and I know one way to get rid of it, to numb my feelings and nerves. So, I do what I do best. I grab the bottle out of my nightstand, shake two pills into my hand, throw them in my mouth, and swallow.

I grab my license, and some cash, from my wallet and shove them in my back pocket. Taking one last look around my room, I open the door and walk out. I know nothing good is going to come of this, but right now I don't care. I need to stop myself from feeling anything.

It's a Saturday night, and there's no shortage of parties to attend. I stop at the first one I see. There are people everywhere, some drunk and some sober. It's perfect for what I need. I head straight for the kitchen. It's not hard to find, the cluster of people is a pretty good indication that I'm going in the right direction.

I pull myself up on one of the counters, trying to avoid sticky spots from spilled beer. I'm not leaving this spot until I can feel the buzz hit my system. I ask someone to get a beer for me. I'm not sure who it is, but soon a red cup is shoved into my hand. It takes me seconds to empty the contents, and I'm asking for another. Placing my hands on either side of me, I graze a glass bottle. I pick it up. It's whiskey, not a brand I've heard of, but it'll do the trick.

Between the beer and whiskey, I'm beginning to feel the oblivion I'm seeking. I hop down from the counter, wobbling. I grasp the edge to steady myself, waiting a couple of seconds before I trust my limbs to carry me to the living room where the music is pumping and bodies are swaying close together.

I insert myself into the crowd, bumping into people and trying to stay upright. I make it to the middle and start dancing. It's not like before, not when Travis had to pull me from a table. I learned a lesson from that, and I don't want to repeat it.

Halfway into the song I feel hands grab my waist from behind. They aren't *his*. I know what those hands feel like after the many times I've been wrapped up in them. I'm turning around to tell the guy behind me to back off, when I'm jostled forward, and his hands are ripped from my body. The room turns to complete chaos.

travis

THIS DAY HAS BEEN SHIT, and seeing some other guy put his hands on my girl makes it a million times worse. Why is she even here? Oh, that's right because I'm an asshole and didn't answer any of her texts or calls. Deep down, I knew what that would do to her. How it would make her feel, but I was hoping that maybe, for once, she wouldn't turn to self-destruction to heal.

We would be on our date right now if it wasn't for the call I received earlier. I planned on taking her to Austin so we could listen to live music and just hang out. But my mom called. I wasn't going to answer it. I told myself not to press the accept icon, but I did. She's in rehab, which is great, don't get me wrong. But, it was the events that led her to being admitted that pissed me off.

She overdosed on who knows what, she won't tell me. But when she was rushed to the hospital, they found prescriptions that didn't belong to her and a large amount of weed. They took her in as soon as she was stable. That was over a week ago. I don't even know where she got the money to buy the drugs, or if she stole them. I wouldn't put it past her. The only reason I even know she's in rehab now is because her therapist told her she needed to inform me. Apparently, the judge gave her a choice, jail time or rehabilitation.

I can't let that be Cami's future. If she keeps doing this anytime something goes wrong, that's where she'll end up. She's better than that. I may be pissed that she's here in the first place, because of me, but I'm not going to let this dude assume he can do whatever he wants because she's drunk.

I don't wait to see how Cami is going to handle the situation, I just react. I shove my way through the crowd of people, not caring who I knock down. I yank him away from Cami, pushing her forward. Spinning him around, I don't even look to see who it is, I don't really care, I start punching.

People are trying to pull me off of him, but I push them away with one arm. Who the hell does he think he is just going up to women and grabbing them? He should show some fucking respect, not that I'm much better with how I handled things with Cami. But still, I don't go around assuming someone will be okay with me putting my hands on them.

There's only one voice that stops me. The only person who can bring some sort of clarity to the moment. "Travis," Cami calls out, just above a whisper.

I stop, immediately, and look over my shoulder. She's curled up, her arms around her legs, and her head resting on her knees. I can see her shoulders shaking, no doubt crying in her bubble. I'm worried I scared her, and she has every right to be afraid. I've never acted like this, but my mom on top of seeing her here, it put me over the edge. Rage and frustration bubbled over, and I needed an outlet.

I look down at the cause of this. He has a bloody nose and lip, and a cut above his eyebrow. "I-I'm sorry, man," he stutters. "I didn't know she was here with anyone."

I help him get to his feet, and straighten my clothes. "It doesn't matter if she was here with someone or not." I spit out. "You don't get to do whatever you want just because she seems like she won't put up a fight. Next time ask the person if they want to dance before you grab them." I shove him away from me. I can't focus on him, Cami needs me.

Bending down, I set my hand on her wrist. "Cami." She looks up at me, tears in her wide eyes. Shit, I did this to her. I made her lose control. I pull her hand away from her leg, and help her up. "Let's go."

I push through the whispering crowd. I'm sure this is going to start some kind of rumor, but I don't care. The more I think of Cami in this situation the more pissed off I get. Not just about that guy, but also the fact that she was here in the first place.

As soon as we're outside the tiny house, she comes to a stop. There are still tears streaming down her face, but she's not scared like she was before. She's glaring at me the way she did when I tried to ask her on our very first date. Why the fuck is she mad at me? All I did was stop some asshole from taking advantage of her.

"What the hell was that?" she screeches and shoves me back.

"What do you mean? I was saving your ass, yet again, from making a bad decision." I yell back.

"If you would have waited two freaking seconds, I was going to handle it." She pauses, gearing up for her next verbal punch. "Besides, I wouldn't have even been here if you hadn't stood me up. Do you have any idea how worried I was before I realized you just didn't fucking care? That I wasn't worth the effort of a simple fucking text saying we needed to cancel."

"I'm sorry, I had a lot on my mind. I didn't think to text you."

"Or respond to my messages, or pick up the damn phone when I called," she pokes me in my chest. "It would have taken less than a minute. That was it, but you couldn't even do that. I let down my walls, and told you about my life. I let you in on my insecurities, and you basically confirmed them tonight."

Cami's pacing now, unable to stay in one place while she lashes out at me. The few people outside of the house are staring at us. I wouldn't be surprised if some of them are recording our fight. I don't care.

"So," I say. "This is your grand plan. Any time things get rocky, you go off the rails and get drunk. Because, you know, that's going to solve everything." She flinches. I know I've hurt her but I don't care. "I didn't respond because shit went down with my mom today. She overdosed over a week ago, and just thought to tell me about it today. I almost fucking lost her. She may have been a shitty mother, but she's still my mom."

Cami pulls to a stop. "I'm sorry, I-I didn't know." She tries to grab my arm, to comfort me, but I shrug her off. I don't need her sympathy, not when she's heading in the same direction.

"Why were you here, then?" she asks. "If you didn't want to be around me, why did you come here?" She's crying again, like this situation is mostly my fault.

"I wasn't coming here intentionally," I sigh, rubbing my forehead. "I needed to think, so I took a walk. I saw you through the kitchen window, and decided to come check on you. Right after I walked in, I saw that guy put his hands on you, and I snapped."

Cami doesn't say anything, just stares at me. I can't do this anymore. I can't keep coming to the rescue of someone who doesn't care enough about herself to stop making the same decisions over and over again.

"Look," I say. "I can't do this anymore. I can't keep wondering if every time something goes wrong, you're going to go party to try to forget. I've dealt with that behavior my entire life. I'm not going to watch someone else I love continuously hurt themselves."

I don't bother waiting to see how my words hit her. I know they caused damage, though. The sob behind me confirms that. I didn't set out to break her heart, but I'm not coming away from this relationship unscathed. I wanted to be the person she leans on. I needed her to make choices that wouldn't destroy her. In the end, we are both fools for thinking we could work this out. She's too much like my mother, and I can't condone her choices.

I call Darcy as I walk away. I'm not going to take her

home this time. She doesn't want to be saved. She's told me that many times, but my foolish heart thought that I'd be different.

"Hello?" Darcy answers, confused.

"Hey, it's Travis. You need to go get Cami." I'm calm and collected, not giving a hint that my heart is shattering into a million pieces. I give her the address and hang up before she says anything else.

When I get home, I pack a bag. I need to go home and see Mom. I'll be back tomorrow, so I shove clothes into my backpack. I want to see her for once in my life. I need to know that she's going to keep getting better. If she can do it, maybe there's hope for Cami.

cami

SOMEONE IS POUNDING on the door, startling me awake. For a second I hope it's Travis, but then his words from last night come tumbling back. *"I can't do this anymore."*

I don't even know how I got home last night. After Travis walked away from me, I went back inside, straight to the kitchen. I didn't even bother with beer from the keg, I went right to the bottle of whiskey I was drinking earlier.

I may have finished off the whiskey, but I'm not sure. Things started to get a little hazy around that point. I vaguely remember Darcy showing up at the party, pissed off, and yelling. But I couldn't hear a word she said.

The banging on the door hasn't stopped. I burrow myself beneath the blankets, trying my hardest to disappear. Whatever is on the other side can't be good.

Finally, the noise stops. I guess Darcy answered it. I roll over, peeking out of my blanket armor, and gasp. It's not who I expected it to be. I assumed Darcy might have called my dad, tired of seeing me like this. But, apparently, she called Tonya.

"Wh-what are you doing here?" I stutter. It's not that I'm unhappy to see her, but the look on her face tells me I'm not going to like what she has to say. And, this is so not the way I wanted her and Darcy to meet.

"Darcy called me," she replies. Her arms are crossed over her chest, and her hip is popped out. She doesn't look amused. It's a stance I've seen her mom do a million times before, usually when we are in major trouble.

"What in the hell is going on, Cami?" she demands. She doesn't give me time to reply, or even open my mouth. "I get a call at one in the morning telling me I need to get down here, and knock some sense into your head."

I turn my head toward Darcy. She's sitting in her desk chair, wringing her hands. "I'm sorry. I didn't know who else to call." She stares at me. "You could barely walk last night. I had to carry most of your weight just getting us home."

My choices are no longer only self-destructive, they are touching those I care about, causing them pain. I sit up in my bed, but I look down at my lap. I can't face the disappointment in their eyes. Or, their judgement.

The foot of the bed dips, and one of my friends grabs my hand. "Do you remember when you said I had to do what made me happy?" Tonya asks. I only nod. "I know the circumstances are different, but does this make you happy? Going out and getting drunk, acting the way you do?"

"Not really," I choke out. "I just don't know how to

deal with everything, my emotions or anxiety. It's the only way I know how to forget and not feel anything."

Tonya sighs. "First thing, when did you start having anxiety issues, and why did I not know?"

I don't know how to tell her how long it's been going on without hurting her feelings for not confiding in her. "Since high school. When my father started putting all that pressure on me, and telling me what I *had* to do with my life. It's gotten worse with the stunts he pulls trying to micromanage me while I'm here."

Now Tonya is sniffling, wiping a tear from her cheek. "Why didn't you tell me? This has been going on for years, and you can't use Layla as an excuse. I've only been handling that for less than a year. We're best friends. I wish you had been comfortable enough to tell me."

Shrugging I say, "I didn't realize that's what it was when we were in high school. I didn't get an actual diagnosis until I came here and went to the school clinic. They prescribed me medicine."

"Does it help?" she asks.

Darcy clears her throat. She knows I don't want to be honest about what I usually do when I take them, but I need to tell Tonya everything. "When I take them the way I'm supposed to, they do."

"What does that mean?" She cocks her head to the side, confusion written all over her face.

I want to bury my face in my blankets, and hope they swallow me whole. "I usually take a couple before I go out and party. It helps me find the buzz more quickly."

"Dammit, Cami," she exclaims. "Don't you know you

could kill yourself doing that? What is that going to prove to your father?" She stands up, trying to get her emotions, and anger, under control. "Look, all that is going to do is show your dad that he's right in controlling every single part of your life. I know you don't want that. This has to stop, now. I won't lose my best friend over stupid decisions made to take the pain away. You'll either take your meds when you need them...the way you're supposed to take them. Or, I'll dispose of them."

She must see the look of horror on my face because she holds up her hand. "I'm not saying this to be a bitch. I love you, and I don't want anything to happen to you. What kind of example are you setting for your niece? Do you want Layla to see you like that?"

That question is what punches me in the stomach. I love that little girl, almost more than I love Tonya. I don't want her to see me in the situations I've gotten myself into. I want to be the cool aunt. But even I know that's not going to happen if I keep falling into oblivion.

Darcy steps in, coming to my rescue. "She actually hasn't been taking her anxiety medication in the past few weeks. She hasn't had a reason to."

"What changed?" Tonya asks.

Darcy is looking at me, urging me to tell Tonya. But I don't want to tell her that Travis was the reason. That I felt safe with him. I shouldn't need a guy to make things easier. Since I don't say anything, Darcy answers. "Travis. He's made her happier." She turns to me again, "What happened last night? I thought y'all had a date."

"Ugh," I moan. "We did. He wasn't answering my calls or messages, so I assumed that he wanted nothing to do with me, like I wasn't good enough for him. I decided to go out, and drown in my sorrows." I take a deep breath. "He saw me when he was passing by the party. He came in to check on me, and about that same time, a guy came up behind me and started dancing with me. Before I had a chance to tell him to 'screw off,' Travis was there and beat the hell out of him."

I stop talking for a bit. My eyes are watering, and I'm choking back the sobs that want to erupt. "We got into a huge fight, and he ended things with me. He said I was too much like his mom, and that he couldn't watch me destroy myself."

There's no stopping the cries passing through my lips, or the tears streaming down my face. I grab my stomach, bending over. I can't breathe. How in the hell did I allow myself to lose one of the few good people in my life? Especially someone that wanted to help me because I was too blind to see that I needed it.

I feel two sets of arms wrap around me, holding me together while I fall apart. I don't know what I did to deserve these ladies in my life, but I'm glad I have them on my side. It's definitely much better than being alone and feeling all of this. With their support, I can do anything.

Suddenly, both of them pull back. I'm still trying to stop the flow of my tears, and hiccupping while catching my breath. I hear my television come on, and the crinkle of the popcorn bag being opened before it's put in the microwave.

Soon the smell of butter, and sounds of Buffy fill the room. Tonya and Darcy are on either side of me.

Tonya leans over, and whispers, "You've taught her well."

I smirk, glancing at Darcy, "She'd never even seen Buffy until a few weeks ago."

Tonya's shocked gasp says more than anything. "That's blasphemous."

I nod, and settle in for yet another binge marathon. This will never get old. I have two of my favorite people surrounding me. The only thing that could make it better is if Travis was here. I'm going to take things one step at a time. I can't be happy with someone else if I'm not happy with my own situation.

It's getting late, and I know Tonya needs to get back home to her family. "Shouldn't you be on your way home already?"

"Nope," she replies. "I'll leave in the morning."

"Who is taking care of Layla?"

"Reaf offered to keep her for the night," she laughs. "But he's at his house with his mom and sister. I know she's in good hands."

"If only you had a camera set up to record his reaction to his first poopy diaper." I can almost picture the freak out. I'm sure it wouldn't be much different than mine. But I'm the aunt, the fun one, I don't change nasty diapers.

"His sister has offered to take video for me." She's setting out the last blanket we need for our bed on the floor. I didn't want to sleep alone, and there wasn't a place for Tonya to sleep. I decided we should make a pallet, and go to bed sleepover style. It reminds me of the nights Tonya and I spent together as children.

We talk about everything and nothing. When their breathing starts to slow, I whisper into the dark. "Thank you, both. I love y'all." I didn't think they heard me, but immediately after I feel both of my hands being grasped with a gentle squeeze. Tomorrow is a new day, and I know what I need to do before I can move forward with my life.

TWENTY

travis

IT'S BARELY BEEN a day since I've spoken to Cami, and I miss her already. I regretted the words I said right after they left my mouth. I could have handled the whole situation better, but I can't keep enabling that sort of behavior. I can't go through the heartbreak over and over again. I just hope she knows that ending things between us is tearing me apart.

She's not in class, again. I can't help but feel like I'm the reason. That I drove her into another downward spiral she may not be able to pull herself out of. I don't want her to end up like my mom.

I can't dwell on thoughts of Cami, though. I'm drained from the long drive to see Mom. She's only been in the rehabilitation center for a week, and already, she looks better than I've ever seen her. The dark circles that used to frame her eyes are slowly receding, and her skin has more color to it. She seemed genuinely happy to see me, something I've never seen before. I was always a pain, something that got in the way of her horrible habit.

When I asked her why rehab, she replied, *"The overdose scared me. I realized I didn't want to die, and I didn't want to miss out on any more of your life."*

Those words broke me. I've waited so, so long to hear her say she cares about me. It took her reaching rock bottom to notice me. As long as she's doing everything she can to stay clean, I'll try to work on my relationship with her. It's not going to happen overnight, there's too much pain and sadness built up over the years for that. But, I'm willing to give her a chance.

Thinking about my mom, I can't help but think of Cami, and her absence. Maybe I should give her a second chance. She's not as far gone as my mom was. Maybe I can help her after all.

Class is finally over. It seems like the further into the year we get the more boring the professor is. Maybe we're all just too excited for the end of the school year that's fast approaching. I would be more excited, but the thought of not seeing a glimpse of Cami for three months is enough to bring me to my knees. The few weeks over winter break were brutal, and we weren't even an item. We're not now, but I'm hoping I can change that.

I pull my phone out of my back pocket, and call Derrick. "What's up?" he answers. I swear he will never learn how to properly answer the phone.

"I have a question," I reply. He doesn't say anything, so I assume that's permission to continue. "If I were to screw things up with Cami, break up with her, and then decide I want to keep trying, would I be making a terrible decision?"

"You and Cami split up?" he gasps in surprise. "What happened? Did she go off the deep end again?"

"Something like that," I run my hand through my hair. "I screwed up, and said a couple of not very nice things to her. Do you think she'll forgive me if I try to apologize?"

"That depends..." he says.

"Depends on what?" I demand.

"What you said to her. Most things can be forgiven. But remember, words can never be forgotten."

"Well, aren't you just a wisdom guru. What the hell should I do, man?" I can hear the desperation in my own voice, and know I sound like a whining child.

"I don't know, why don't you ask her crabby roommate?" He answers. "I wasn't there, and I don't know Cami that well. She'll probably have better answers than me."

"Fine," I mutter. "I'll go talk to Darcy." I don't give him a chance to respond before I hang up. I wish I knew what the full story was between him and Darcy. It just doesn't seem like him annoying her is the whole reason they have so much animosity toward each other. I'll get to the bottom of that whole situation later. Right now, I have my own relationship problems to deal with.

My next class is in thirty minutes. That should give me plenty of time to run over to Cami's dorm. I hope she's there, and that I don't lose my nerve to tell her all that I need to say. The walk over is nice. The sun is shining, but it's not too hot. Flowers along the pathways are in full bloom, and students are lounging all over the lawn. It's the perfect image most colleges give you on their brochures. If only I felt as happy as the scene appears.

I yank open the front door to the recreation area, the RA is nowhere in sight. I take advantage of this and dart toward the stairs. I don't want to wait forever on the elevator. She could come back, and kick me out. Or she could call up to Cami's room, only to inform me she's refused my request to see her.

When I get to Cami's room, I'm breathing hard. I set my hands on my knees, bend over, and try to catch my breath. I don't want to look like an insane person when she opens the door. Finally, when my breathing is under control, and I'm no longer gasping, I knock on the door. Then, I wait.

It takes a few minutes for the door to open, but the person on the other side isn't Cami. It's Darcy, and she looks very annoyed. "What do you need, Travis?"

"Where's Cami? I need to talk to her," I say in one breath. It will be a miracle if she understands anything I just said. But I *need* to see her, talk to her.

Darcy is leaning against the door frame, arms crossed, and staring at me pointedly. "She's not here."

"What do you mean she's not here?" I ask, frantic.

She rolls her eyes, and backs up, letting me enter the room. "I mean she's not here. She went home for a couple of days."

Why on earth would she go home to the people she dislikes more than anyone? I can't see her running to her father's arms to get over a relationship. "Why, and when will she be back?"

Darcy puts her hand on my back, slowly ushering me

toward the still open door. "She has a few unresolved issues she has to work out." Before letting me reply, she shuts the door in my face. No goodbye, just a solid piece of wood inches from my nose.

I still have time to make it to my class, but decide to skip it. Darcy didn't say Cami wasn't coming back to school. I have plans to make to get my girl back.

cami

I STARTED PACKING about an hour after Tonya left. There's only one way I can get past my issues and begin healing. I have to talk to my parents, let them know how I feel and what I've been going through. The worst they can do is disown me. Honestly, it's not something I'm afraid of anymore. I'll figure out how to manage everything on my own.

The drive takes forever. I always forget just how far Hilltown is from home. Instead of letting my anxiety take over, I play Ed Sheeran the entire time. His voice soothes my soul. I'd normally listen to heavy metal when I have to have any kind of conversation with my parents. But today, I need clarity. If I have any hope of them actually listening to me, I need to be calm and collected.

The only problem with listening to Ed Sheeran is the love songs. Almost all of them talk about romance in some form. It makes it hard for my mind not to wander to Travis. Is there a possibility for us in the future? That's part of the reason I'm going home. In order for me to move forward with my life, I need to stop carrying the pressures of my family. I also need to stop letting my reactions to things I can't control interfere with the people I care about.

Saturday night was a game changer. I not only let down my friends, I disappointed Travis. I took him to a place he's relived many times throughout his childhood. I didn't care if I hurt him. All I cared about was myself, and my feelings. I don't think I will ever forget the pain and betrayal I saw in his eyes, and I was the cause of it. I made him doubt me, and doubt us. I just hope it's not too late for me to make it up to him. To prove to him that I can change, and all I need is a second chance.

It's just after three in the afternoon when I pull into my parent's driveway. Funny how I no longer think of this house as mine. If I'm being honest it stopped being *home* when I was in high school. I always spent as much time as I could at Tonya's house to avoid my father.

The house is massive for only three people, two stories with five bedrooms. I'm not going to lie, I never had a bad childhood. It just never felt like a true family. We weren't the sort to have game nights, or really do anything together. The only time we ever saw each other was when we had dinner, or an event at my father's firm. Otherwise, we kept to ourselves. As long as I didn't step over the line there was no need to call a "family meeting" to gripe about my actions.

I knock on the door, that's how out of place I feel in the house I grew up in. It takes a few moments for my mother to answer. "Cami," she utters. "What are you doing here? Shouldn't you be in school?"

I play with the edges of my shirt, looking down. I know I need to be confident, but I can already feel the anxiety clawing up my spine. "Yes, but I need to talk to you and Dad."

Mom ushers me in, reminding me to take my shoes off before entering the rest of the house. Always so prim and proper, even when she can tell there's something going on with her daughter. She can sense my unease, it's practically seeping through my pores. Walking me to the living room, she motions for me to take a seat on the sofa. "Would you like something to drink?"

I shake my head. My surprise visit has thrown her off. She doesn't know how to act around me if it's not on their terms. I know she loves me, but maybe she'll stand up for me for once. "Let me go get your father."

I'm left sitting in the living room by myself. I look around and take in the fact that although they live here, this house doesn't look lived in. The furniture and decorations look like something straight out of a magazine. What others aspire to have their homes look like, even though they'll never actually use the rooms.

I hear heavy footfalls coming down the hall. He's always been one to make his presence known before entering a room. I think he uses it as an intimidation technique, a way to make his clients, or me, sweat before he swoops in. He doesn't even bother greeting me. "Why aren't you at school?"

"I-I need to talk to you," I push the words past my lips. Already I can feel my determination slip. But I remember the look Travis gave me, and the fear in Tonya and Darcy's eyes, and I strengthen my resolve. "We need to discuss my future."

"You better not be here to tell me you're knocked up," he demands. "I always knew that Tonya girl would be a bad influence on you."

I stand up, quick to defend my best friend and the only person who has honestly given a damn about me. "That's where you're wrong. She has never been a bad influence. If anything, she's shown me what it's like to have a family that cares and shows concern. And no, *Father*, I'm not pregnant."

"Then what is this about," he huffs before taking a seat in the recliner. The only out of place piece of furniture in this room. It's the one thing he wouldn't let Mom get rid of when she redecorated the house.

"I don't want to major in accounting." I blurt out. I planned on doing this a little more eloquently, but maybe it's best to get it all out there at once. "I'm not sure what I want to pursue, but it's definitely not that. I'm not happy doing it, and I'm not happy with you trying to control every aspect of my life."

"Well, Cami, that's just too bad seeing as how I pay for your education." He leans back in his chair, crosses his legs, thinking he's won this battle.

"You won't be after this semester," I reply, grinning. He doesn't know all the research I've done to ensure that I won't have to count on a single penny from him. Hell, he doesn't even know that I've gotten a part time job.

"What does that mean? There's no way you can pay for tuition, let alone afford it," he argues, a smug smirk crossing his face.

"Actually, I can." I say. "See, I got a job a few weeks ago. It doesn't pay much, but it helps. I've also looked into, and applied, for scholarships and grant programs for the next semester." I see his resolve fall away. He's not sure whether to believe me, or insist I'm bluffing.

"I won't allow that. How can you work while going to school? You aren't mature enough, Cami. I refuse to let this happen." He's standing up now, pacing the floor. His face is beet red, and I can practically see steam coming off the top of his head.

"Honey," Mom steps in, "Maybe we should listen to her. We don't want her to resent us for the rest of our lives."

"I don't care if she hates us," he yells. "She is going to do what she's been told, and not act like some defiant child."

I love how he talks about me like I'm not even in the room. Like I'm not worth the effort of having a real conversation. No wonder I suck at relationships. I've had such an awesome example growing up with this man.

"That's enough," I exclaim. I'm sure I'm turning as red as he is. But I can't keep the anger out of my voice. "Last time I checked, I'm an adult. I don't want the life you have planned out for me, and I'm not going to keep heading down that path." Tears are welling up in my eyes. I don't care, maybe if he sees how much it affects me, he'll finally see where I'm coming from. "I'm changing my major next semester, with or without your blessing."

"Then, young lady, you can do it without my money and without my house to come home to when you are on break." He crosses his arms, staring me down. "You will be cut off, from everything."

I sag in defeat. I was hoping maybe he would *see* me. See how much I loathe accounting. But, as usual, he only sees what he wants to see. To him, I'll always be a child. Someone he can push around. "Fine, Dad. Have it your way. I won't be seeing you when I leave school next month. If you don't want to even try compromising, then I'm forced to do it on my own. I hope you're happy now."

I turn to leave the room. My father is stammering in the background, trying to find the words that will keep me under his thumb. Unfortunately for him, there aren't any. I've made my decision. I've cut the one toxic person, that has had a hold on me for far too long, out of my life. Before walking to the entryway to collect my shoes, I stop and hug my mom. "Thank you for at least trying to step in. You don't know what it means to me." She gives me one last squeeze. I look up and see a tear slip from her eye. At least I'll have her on my side no matter what happens.

As soon as I get in my car, I breathe a sigh of relief. I finally stood up for myself. The sense of freedom is short-lived, though. I need to figure out where I'm going to stay when I come back next month.

I back out of the driveway, and head in the direction where I've always felt safe. The family who has always been there for me when I needed them. I'm about to crash dinner.

I knock on Tonya's door, bouncing on my toes. Her mom opens the door, and the moment she notices that it's me, brings me in for a long hug. "Can't breathe," I gasp. She's laughing and crying, not sure which emotion is going to win out. I guess that means Tonya told them about my shenanigans.

"Oh, Cami," Mama B whispers. "I'm so happy to see you. Are you hungry? You look hungry, go to the kitchen." I love how even though I'm barging in on them, she's always prepared to welcome me with open arms, literally.

I can smell the spices as I walk toward the kitchen. Dinner here is always my favorite. It doesn't matter what they're cooking, or if I'll even like it. It's the experience. It's knowing that no matter what, I'll be accepted. That I'll be brought into the fold like I'm part of the family.

Everyone is seated around the table, including Reaf. I make quick introductions and take the empty seat beside Tonya, ready to dig in. The fresh tortillas are calling my name. Tonya glances at me and nods. She knows I did what I came here to do. She also knows that I'm going to need her support and kindness more than ever.

Small talk erupts around the small table, and everyone is saying how their day was. When there's a lull, I clear my throat, swallowing the food I had in my mouth. "I know you already have a full house, but my father just cut me off and said I can't come back when school releases next month. Is there any way I could maybe stay here for the summer?" I make sure I pull out the puppy dog eyes and bat my lashes. I know they won't tell me no, but I have to up my cuteness game. "I'll get a job when I get here, and pay rent. So you won't have to worry about supporting me."

Mama B laughs. I wasn't expecting that. "Of course,

you don't even have to ask. You practically live here when you're home anyway. Besides, I think Layla would enjoy having you around."

"Thank you, so much." I'm on the verge of crying, yet again. I didn't know my body could produce more tears. "You'll never even know I'm here."

This time Tonya's dad speaks up, "You know that doesn't fly around here. If you're here, you're a part of the family. You always have been, and always will be."

When I leave the next morning, I feel lighter than I have in years. My heart is full, and I even got to cuddle with my little Layla. Things are starting to look up. I just need to fix one more thing before school lets out for the summer.

travis

I DIDN'T BOTHER LOOKING for Cami yesterday. Darcy said she would be gone for a couple of days. I was surprised to see Cami sitting in her usual desk in the back row when I walked into class today. I didn't expect her back so soon. But I breathe a sigh of relief seeing her there.

Now if only I can work up the courage to speak to her. Things will definitely be strained between us for a while, if she'll even talk to me. I'm praying she will. I have a plan that includes groveling, but I'm going to need the same from her. She was in the wrong, too.

When class is over, she walks out of the classroom as fast as she can. I guess right now isn't going to be the time for our confrontation. I'm not upset about it. I don't really want to have this conversation in front of most of the student body.

I go about the rest of my day, going to class, and running through everything I want to say to her. I've practiced my speech so many times, I should have it memorized, but I know I'm going to fumble over the words when I come face to face with her.

Before I go back to my room, I walk to Roasted. I'm going to need a caffeine boost to get through the mounds of homework my professors assigned. I think they save it all up until right before summer break to make us insane. It's like a test to see if we'll be able to become full functioning adults. I don't know what all this will prove, it's not like we'll use most of this information in real life. But then again, we might, if we choose to go into that field of study for our careers. I'm not very concerned about that right now, though. I still haven't found anything that clicks. I just hope I do before the end of the Fall semester.

I open the door, and almost turn around. Cami is behind the counter. She has her hair pulled up in a messy bun, and she's wearing her Roasted uniform; black pants and t-shirt with the logo printed on the right side. She's stunning, and I don't even think she realizes it. She's smiling, and I feel like it's been forever since I've seen her face filled with so much joy. It gives me hope that we can work through our circumstances.

I stand in the line of people ahead of me, antsy to get to the front. I just want to be in her proximity, even if she never wants to speak to me again. Finally, I'm in front of her. I lean against the counter, much like Derrick did the first time I brought him here, trying to exude confidence.

She looks up from the register and her eyes widen. "Hi," she says. "What can I get you today?" She's playing with a piece of hair that's fallen from her bun, a clear sign that she's nervous.

"How about a date?" I ask, half kidding. When her

smile falters just a little I change course. "Just a coffee, black." She's entering the order in on the computer, doing anything she can to avoid looking at me. "Cami, can we talk?" I ask.

She pauses before telling me the total. She takes a deep breath, and lets it out. "Yeah. I get off at eight. Do you want to meet me at my dorm? We have a lot to discuss."

"Yes," I exhale. Knowing I'll get to see her in a few short hours, alone, gives me hope. I give her my money, and place the change in the tip jar. "I'll see you later." I walk to the end of the counter, pick up my order, and walk out of the shop. I take one last look through the window, and see her staring at me. I just hope we can forgive each other for the awful things we've said.

* * *

I'm knocking on her door once again. It's nine at night, and I'm anxious to see her. I decided to give her a bit to get cleaned up before I came over. The RA didn't even bat an eye when I walked straight to the elevator. I guess she's accepted the fact that I'm going to be around for a while.

I half expect Darcy to answer the door saying that Cami doesn't want to see me, but it's not her. Cami is standing in front of me, and it's taking everything in me not to sweep her into my arms. "Hi," I wave. I feel like a dumbass for waving, but I don't know what to do with my hands.

She motions me in and over to her bed. I sit on the

edge, trying not to get too comfortable in case this goes South. She climbs up and puts a pillow in her lap, a barrier for her when she's feeling vulnerable.

"I'm sorry," we both say at once. Cami lets out a small laugh. "You go first," I tell her.

She sighs, searching for the right words. "I'm sorry. I acted like a huge bitch toward you, and said some pretty mean things. I didn't mean to take out my anger on you."

"It's okay," I say. "I didn't exactly say the best things to you either. I was just terrified that you would end up hurting yourself, and I don't want to see you in pain. Not when you can come to me."

"I know." She runs her fingers back and forth over the pillow, doing whatever she can to keep from looking at me, like she's ashamed. "I let my insecurities get to me when you didn't show up and didn't answer my calls. I didn't know what else to do. But Tonya came here the next day, and chewed my ass out in the nicest way possible. I don't want to be like that. Not with you, my friends, or Tonya's sweet little baby."

She looks up at me, tears in her eyes. "I went home Monday, after Tonya left, to try to talk some sense into my dad, and tell him how I feel. It didn't change anything, except for being disowned." I'm about to interrupt her, but she keeps going. "And it's okay. I'm good with his decision. I can do this, whether it's with his support or not. I just don't want to disappoint the people I care about."

The look in her eyes tells me I'm included in that group of people. That she considers me important, and that fills my heart more than possibly anything else. "I went home, too. I had to see my mom. To see if she's really going to make better choices." I'm playing with a hole in my jeans because, again, I don't know what to do with my hands. "She's doing good. She was scared that she ruined things forever. We're going to work on our whole mother-son relationship and see what happens. But she's staying in rehab until the judge deems her okay to release."

She throws her arms around me, "That's great. I'm happy to hear your mom is okay. I've been worried since you told me."

I can't keep my arms from bringing her closer. I stroke her hair with one hand, while the other is placed at the small of her back. "I care about you, Cami, a lot. Hell, I'm falling in love with you. But, you have to promise me that when things get to be too much, you'll come to me. I'll help you find the beauty in the cruelty, and the happiness in the darkness. I just need you to come to *me* instead of turning to alcohol. Can you do that? For us?"

"Yes," she mutters into my neck. She leans back just enough to look me in the eyes. "But you have to come to me too. If things with your mom start to get to you, I want you to let me be the one that helps you through it."

You would think I won the lottery with the smile that takes over my face. I'm sure I look like Joker, but nicer. "Deal." I pull her back into my arms and savor this moment I never thought I would get. We've compromised, and that's all I could ever ask for. This woman in front of me has me, heart and soul.

epilogue

One month later

I CLOSE the trunk of my car. Who knew I could accumulate so much crap within such a short period of time? It's almost bitter sweet leaving the campus today. It's time for summer break, and so much has happened these past five months. I'm definitely not the person I was at the beginning of the semester.

Next semester I'll be juggling working with my class load, but I can do it. I have faith in myself, and I know a few people that will keep me in line. I wouldn't have made it through this school year without a badass support system.

I was shocked my phone was still working after I left my parent's house. I assumed my father would have canceled the plan as soon as I walked out of the house. I guess I have my mom to thank for that. At least I have her support. She may not be very affectionate, but the small things let me know that she is still fighting for me.

I haven't talked to Dad since our argument. He may need time to calm down and get his head out of his ass. But I'm not bowing down, I'm going to continue moving forward with whatever makes me happy. Maybe I'll keep sketching, or maybe I'll be a doctor. Who knows? I have time to figure it out.

I'm definitely happy that I'll be able to see Travis over the summer. He lives in Dallas, which is only forty-five minutes from me. A long distance relationship would have pushed me to the edge, but we would have made it work. I'll be working at Brew's Clues while I'm staying with Tonya and her family. I really like working in a coffee shop, despite the smelling like coffee beans when I leave. And yes, Brew's Clues is a play on that kid's television show, big red chair and everything. I'm excited to spend my summer with my best friend and niece. And I guess Reaf, too, since he's almost always where Tonya is.

Travis walks out of my dorm, carrying one last box of clothes. "I think this is it. Will it fit in your car?"

I shake my head. "Doubt it. I don't think I could fit a sandwich bag in the trunk."

"It's okay, I'll just put it in my back seat. I don't have nearly as much stuff as you. Do you even use everything you have in here?" He asks, quirking an eyebrow.

I swat at his arm before kissing his cheek. "A girl has to have options. I may need something in that box at any given time."

He laughs and places the box in his car. He's right, his SUV isn't nearly as full as my car. But I'm going to chalk that up to him having a bigger vehicle. He closes the door and sweeps me into his arms, spinning me around. He kisses my forehead and the tip of my nose before finally finding his way to my lips. I love that his kisses are sweet and tender. He doesn't push for more. I wrap my arms around him, deepening the kiss, our tongues swirling together. I gently bite his bottom lip before pulling away, and running to my car.

He beats me by a couple of seconds, and already has my car door open, waiting for me to get in. I slide into the driver seat, and before he closes it, he presses one more kiss to my mouth. "I'll follow you to Tonya's. I'm excited to meet the one person who can talk some sense into that thick skull of yours."

"Hey," I bat his hands away from my head. "You've talked plenty of sense into me."

"You're damn right," he replies before closing the door.

I start my car, and wonder what lies ahead of me. Life may not be fair or easy, but with my friends and Travis on my side, I can find my way through this cruel and beautiful world.

* * *

Prologue

The streets of Asheville are bustling. People are walking down the street staring into shop windows as if they don't have a care in the world. I wish I could say the same. I wish guilt didn't eat away at me, especially now, as I watch Tonya and Reaf walking down the sidewalk holding hands.

That should be me. I should be the one with my arms wrapped around Tonya and focusing on our baby girl. But...she chose him. I can understand why, but it doesn't stop the jealousy from bubbling up in my gut. It doesn't keep the anger from rising to the surface. I knew what I would see if I came home from school, but I still decided to come back and torture myself by watching them together. Asheville is a small town, and there's no way I would be able to avoid them completely.

Tonya and Reaf stroll down Main Street, glancing through shop windows, pushing a stroller in front of them. A stroller that holds my child. My beautiful baby girl, Layla. I really don't have any right to call her mine. I mean, she is biologically, but I haven't been here for her or Tonya. At least, not in any way that put me in a good light. I gave up that right when I asked Tonya to give me time to adjust to the knowledge that I have a child.

They stop in front of a baby boutique, hands pressed to their foreheads, trying to see through the glare in the window. Reaf bends down, and when he stands up again, he has Layla cuddled up against his chest. I don't know what they are shopping for, but I'm not a fan of how cozy they look together.

I clench my hands together until they are curled into fists. I can feel my face heating, and my breathing is becoming labored. I'm struggling to get my anger under control, but it's hard. I shouldn't be this enraged, but that's my kid he's holding. My kid he's playing father to.

I quickly turn the corner putting them out of my line of sight. I need to calm down, but I know seeing them together, as a *family*, isn't going to accomplish anything.

I shouldn't have come back. I could be in my dorm right now playing Madden with the guys. But, no...I'm storming off like a fucking child because I can't handle the repercussions of my decision to not be in Layla's life yet.

I wasn't ready for that responsibility. Hell, I'm still not ready but I want to be. Not only for Layla but for myself. I want to have the strength to do this whole co-parenting thing that Tonya kept on about.

I shove my way through people milling about enjoying their Spring day, while I'm in turmoil. I'm pretty sure I hear someone holler my name, but I don't turn around. If Tonya is chasing after me, I won't be able to handle it.

Finally seeing the outline of my car, I pick up the pace. Hitting the key fob at the same time as I grab the handle, I yank the door open and slide into the car. I check both ways before pulling out of the parking spot and into traffic.

In my rearview mirror I see Tonya standing at the edge of the sidewalk disbelief written all over her face. I feel a stab of guilt that I've hurt her once again, but there's nothing I can do about it. I'm going to run home, grab my stuff and head back to the dorms. I'm not ready to face this.

Pick up your copy of *Ways to Go*.

acknowledgments

This part of the book is always the hardest to write. I have so many people that help me on this crazy, and amazing journey. Nessa, your go-getter attitude, and faith, that I could finish this book by the deadline is what made me get my ass in front of the computer and write. I seriously don't know what I would do without you, Bestie.

My Alpha readers, you guys are fucking rockstars! Jennifer, Cynthia, Mistee, Carine, and Kristin; your input while writing was phenomenal. You helped me shape this story, and caught all of my horrible typing errors. Thank you for your excitement, and reading every time I messaged you that a new chapter was available. I'm sorry I made y'all cry. (Not really, that's my job.)

My beta readers: Ariel, Erica, and Stephanie; thank you for catching anything else. Your input is always helpful, and I can't wait to bug y'all with another story.

Shelly at Small Edits, thank you for polishing Cami's story and just being freaking amazing. Crystal, at KP Designs, thank you an amazing cover.

My Sisterhood ladies, sorry I was away for a while, but your posts always keep me sane. I fucking love y'all. Stay awesome, Sisters!

To my mom and dad, thank you for your unwavering

support. I couldn't do this without y'all on my side. Mom, I'm sorry for peppering you with a thousand questions, and thank you for not rolling your eyes too much. Dad, thanks for being there and listening to all of my excitement over numbers and rankings. It's the little things that count.

And to my amazing, little family, thank you for being you and believing Mommy can do this whole writing thing. And thank you for picking up the slack when I had my fingers on the keyboard. You're pretty awesome people. Hubs, Boy Child, and Wee One, y'all make everything better. Boy Child and Wee One, never be afraid to chase your dreams.

Finally, bloggers and readers, thank you for taking a chance on a newbie author. Your words and excitement make this whole gig worth it.

also by katrina marie

The Taking Chances Series

Welcome to Your Life

Cruel and Beautiful World

Ways to Go

Remember That Night

My Only Wish is You

From This Moment

Shoot Down the Stars

Love Will Save Your Soul

Take a Chance

Cousins Gone RomCom Series

Cocky Hero Club

Big Baller

Silverwood Bulldog Series

Baseball & Broadway

Katrina Marie lives in the Dallas area with her husband, two children, and fur baby. She is a lover of all things geeky and Gryffindor for life. When she's not writing you can find her at her children's sporting events, or curled up reading a book.

You can find Katrina Marie online in the following places:

Sign up for my newsletter for extras from Welcome to Your Life: http://bit.ly/2BlDSsZ

Website: katrinamarieauthor.com

facebook.com/KatrinaMarieAuthor

twitter.com/katmarieauthor

instagram.com/katrinamarieauthor

bookbub.com/profile/katrina-marie

pinterest.com/katrinamarieauthor